THE HEART OF WINTER

A Wicked Holidays Novel

RIZZO ROSE

This is a work of fiction. All of the characters, organizations, and events portrayed in these stories are either products of the author's imaginations or are used fictitiously and are not construed as real. Any resemblance to actual events, locales, organizations, or persons, living or dead, is entirely coincidental.

Copyright © 2021 by Condor & Hart LLC

All rights reserved. This book or any portion thereof may not be reproduced or used in any manner whatsoever without the express written permission of the author or publisher except for the use of brief quotations in a book review.

Cover photo by Period Images

Cover design by Spellcaster Designs

First edition of all titles: December 2021

Print edition ISBN: 978-1-957329-01-7
Digital edition ISBN: 978-1-957329-00-0

For everyone who has ever wanted to smash Santa Claus.

I
ALEXANDER

On the night before his brother's coronation, Alexander Nikolas, Prince of the Eternal Winter Forest, Sword of the Realm, and known thief of hearts was fucking.

For the week leading up to the winter solstice and coronation, every single soul in the kingdom had flocked to the palace to dance and drink frostberry wine in the marbled ballrooms. They ran through the hedge maze in the snow-dusted palace gardens, chasing lovers into dark, delightful corners.

Down in the village, they packed the taverns in Solaris Square and bought gifts of unity and goodness to exchange at midnight on the solstice. They splurged on dresses and tailcoats on the mere chance that they'd be in the presence of the new king—the new Saint Nikolas.

Alexander wanted no part of the merriment and feasting because Alexander didn't care about unity or goodness. Alexander wasn't good. Not in the way he was expected to be. The Eternal Winter Forest was his cage, and every year, every *single* year when the villagers and farmers and the bleeding hearts that populated their isolated little realm gathered to celebrate the legacy of Saint Nikolas, he was forced to listen to his family spout lies. Empty promises.

And yet, Alexander remained the sword, sworn to the crown his eldest brother was born to wear. Perhaps once he'd been expected to be different, but by age thirty-five, all that was asked of Alexander was loyalty and a good time. He might have been descended from a saint, but he had the appetite of a sinner.

Which is precisely why, when he should have been listening to endless speeches, he found himself with a maiden straddling his cock.

"You're *so* good at that, my prince," she moaned.

She had hair like the polished gold leaf trimming every inch of the grand palace. Long curls bounced along with her generous breasts. It was a far better sight than the banquet where he was supposed to be.

Alexander shut his eyes and lost himself to the sensation of being inside her tight cunt. He deserved a bit of fun. It *had* been a horrid week of preparations and decorations and every other frivolous tasks the Master of Revels could concoct.

To his credit, Alexander had attempted to be present at the council meetings and frock fittings. But his thin tolerance for his family had reached its breaking point shortly before the banquet celebration. Alexander could pinpoint the exact moment.

He'd been waiting for his brothers at the closed mahogany doors. Harps and trumpets exhaled in the distance. Alexander tugged on the sleeves of his scarlet tailcoat. He was in ceremonial dress, his lapel decorated with baubles and medals he hadn't earned. The long sword strapped to his hip had never seen combat, outside of the training yards, of course. But it was impressive, gleaming metal and enchanted runes of protection.

"Ah, he's early," Hans said. "It's a great solstice miracle."

Alexander set his jaw and bowed slightly at his older brother. Hans, the Master of Alchemy, resembled a gold statue come to life. His thick, golden hair was always fixed like a cresting wave, and his blue eyes gleamed with a dangerous light, like he'd set the Elfenhörn Forest aflame on a whim because he could get away with it.

"Unlike you," Alexander said, standing straighter because the only thing Hans was self-conscious of was his height, "I decided not to spend hours dressing up like a tinsel soldier."

Hans flashed a crooked smile. His tanned cheeks were dusted with golden freckles from his frequent riding through the evergreen fields. He reached out and placed his long index finger on Alexander's shoulder.

Alexander tried to reel back, but too late. The air sparked with Hans's magic. Blessed with the alchemical ability to transform matter, Hans used his Saint-given gift to turn his youngest brother's suit completely gold to match his own. The silk threads of Alexander's frock shimmered from red to gold like the scales of a fish.

He grabbed Hans by the front of his collar and slammed him against the nearest wall. "Fix it. *Now*."

"I'm merely proving a point, brother," Hans said, laughing.

Alexander growled. "*Fix* it."

"Your sense of humor is always horrid this time of year."

"*Enough*." Wilhelm's baritone command was laced with real threat as he rounded the corner.

In moments, Alexander let go of Hans, and Hans returned Alexander's ceremonial suit back to its deep blood hue.

Wilhelm and Alexander shared the marbled amber eyes of their patron saint, perhaps the only trait that assured Alexander he was indeed his deceased father's son and not the bastard some at the palace liked to whisper. The future king had opted for the more traditional ceremonial garb. Trousers fitted to his brawny legs. A fur-lined cape fastened at his throat with a glistening diamond. His muscular torso was bare, showcasing the Mark of the Saint—an inky brand that started at the hearts of his palms and snaked up his arms like wild ivy and thorns, winding over his shoulders, his pectorals, and stopped just above his heart. The Mark had taken root in Wilhelm on the day their father passed and slowly grew every time he used his gifts. On the night of the solstice, the Mark would be complete.

The heirs of King Nikolas XV stood in the hall of the grand palace, glowering at one another. Wilhelm, the first-born, the crown prince, the true heir of the Mark of the Saint. Hans, middle-born, golden son, and gifted with the power of alchemy. And then there was the youngest, the Sword of the Realm, the spare.

Sometimes Alexander wondered how they shared the same blood. The blood of Saint Nikolas of Myra. A man who had left the known world to create a hidden paradise, free of sin, free of the evils of humanity. The Eternal Winter Kingdom had been his dream, and Alexander and his brothers were the bearers of that legacy.

"Where is your future queen?" Hans asked, adjusting his silk cravat.

Wilhelm's eyebrows shot up in surprise, like he hadn't considered the whereabouts of his wife that day. "Fussing at Everlane I'm sure."

"I'm sure," Hans muttered.

Wilhelm had their father's cold smile, sharp like the curve of a scythe. "I thank you for your concern."

Even Hans had common sense to not respond.

"Now, listen to me very carefully," Wilhelm said, positioning himself before the seam of the doors. He turned his head and held Alexander's irritated stare. "Do not embarrass me the way you did at Father's funeral."

All Alexander had done was set their father's palomino free. How could he have known the stubborn horse was going to ride right into the cathedral during Wilhelm's speech?

"How about I behave," Alexander said, "the day you give a speech that doesn't bore me to death?"

Hans bit down on an involuntary smile and looked at his feet. Wilhelm cleared his throat and stared straight ahead.

"You're so glib for someone born a mistake."

Anger sliced through Alexander. He'd grown up hearing that. *Mistake. Spare. Useless.* After all, he was the sword to the crown. He'd been trained to wield a blade in a kingdom that had known peace for over two centuries. He *hated* the words because deep down, Alexander knew they were right. His brothers always knew how best to cut Alexander to the quick.

Rid of their humor, the brothers flanked their future king and entered the banquet hall. Wilhelm and Hans had perfected the transformation of their public faces. It was like they donned invisible armor when they performed royal duties. They accepted the fawning complements and adoration, the cooing and air-kisses, and took their seats at the head of the enormous mahogany table set for two dozen people lucky enough to have the new king's favor.

Instead of taking his place to the left of Hans, Alexander kept on walking until he reached the other end of the banquet table. Only the brothers noticed Wilhelm's eyebrow tick with displeasure at the slight.

Alexander summoned the well of his charm. Just because he hated the winter solstice, and just because he believed his family legacy was a farce, did not mean the people around him needed to suffer. He plopped into his seat at the far end of the table. He shook hands with Everlane, the Master of Revels, who was nearly falling asleep into the salmon tartare. He asked after the Royal Scholar's litter. He accepted the adoring winks from nearby matrons with cheeks flushed from frostberry wine.

It wasn't *all* bad. The palace was never as beautiful as when it was decked with pine garlands across the archways. Glass chandeliers twinkled with candlelight. Tapers raced to burn down to the wick in extravagant centerpieces of blown glass twisted in the shape of ivy and pale purple currants. There was always music, harps haunting his dead mother's favorite songs through the corridors.

It wasn't all bad, and yet, with all the people, all the chatter, Alexander felt like he couldn't breathe. He grabbed his glass goblet and drank deeply, distantly aware that Wilhelm had begun to rhapsodize about the new age of the realm. Down at their corner of the table the Royal Scholar speculated it meant new schools in the outskirt villages. Meanwhile, the Master of Agriculture suggested Prince Hansel would revive the over-farmed fields in the west.

Fools, Alexander thought.

The winter solstice festivals revived the hope and spirit of the kingdom. Every soul in the land made a pilgrimage to the palace to ask a gift from the king, the marked saint. Their hope hung on a thread the entire year while the palace reveled year-round and ignored the people. Until the solstice.

Fools, Alexander thought again. If his father hadn't granted those wishes—why would his heir?

Deep down. Deep *deep* down, Alexander had hopes that Wilhelm would be a better king than their father. But it was too much to hope.

Another cup, another refill.

And so, when his eyes fell on the wheat-haired maiden at his side, Alexander distracted himself from the politics and speculations of a future he was helpless to change. He was, after all, only the spare.

"My prince," the maiden said. "I am—"

He couldn't hear her over the feast's cacophony. His thoughts dubbed her Sweet Maiden. "And I am charmed."

"Really?" She narrowed canny eyes at him. "You seem as though the festival is not to your liking."

"Ah, but with you at my side, it has improved tenfold."

She leaned against him and whispered, "Why stop at tenfold?"

Under the table, she smoothed her palm up along his thigh and undid the considerable number of silver buttons on his trousers. She unsheathed his hardening cock, and he suppressed a groan as she fisted his length, moving in a steady rhythm that caught him off guard.

He leaned forward, slamming his goblet on the table hard enough to break the stem. The dregs of his wine ran in a thin line on the tablecloth, seeping into the white fabric like blood.

"Are you all right, my prince?" Everlane asked.

Alexander rested his chin on his fist and breathed through the shock of pleasure that ran through him. "Better with every stroke of the clock."

"Tomorrow is going to go down in the records as the greatest solstice in the history of the Eternal Winter Forest," said Elowen.

"Elowen!" someone said. "Shouldn't you be at the Path?"

"Ah, but tonight's the one day that I can leave my post, and I'm going to enjoy myself," Elowen said, shoveling herbed potatoes and lamb into her mouth.

If Alexander hadn't been so distracted, he would have laughed. He enjoyed the Guardian's company more than that of her brothers. But the Sweet Maiden gave him a few more delicious strokes he could not ignore.

He turned his attention back to her and brushed her silky hair behind her gently pointed ear, marking her elfen-blood. He stifled a groan as her thumb circled the wet tip of his cock and sent a tremble down his legs. He gripped the table, and it shook slightly.

The Sweet Maiden's lips tugged at the corner. "Should I stop, Your Highness?"

Alexander leaned into her ear, skimming a kiss there. "Don't you fucking dare."

At the other end of the table, he could feel Wilhelm's disapproving stare. He ignored it and braced his hand on the table as the Sweet Maiden quickened her pace. All around them the feast boomed, the table filled with roasted lamb, succulent quail, golden beets drizzled with honey and topped with crumbled goat cheese.

But Alexander focused on his dinner partner's adoring eyes, the strength of her grip, the coil of pleasure that hooked deep in his balls and spread until he came, and all he heard was her delighted laughter and the pop of sparkling cider overflowing from green bottles.

The Sweet Maiden wiped her hands on a cloth and looked at him. "Pity it all went to waste."

Beside her, Elowen, too busy to notice anything but the troth of plenty, waved down a waiter. "Worry not, there's plenty more pudding, I'm sure."

The Sweet Maiden and Alexander shared a secret smile. He wasn't *usually* one for public displays. He was, however, an eternal student of pleasure, and he wanted to give her what she needed. It was incredibly convenient that what she had needed was to stroke his cock under the table. And now it was his turn to return the favor.

Anything.

Anything to distract him from the gilded farce that was the winter solstice. Instead of celebrating his brother, he'd chosen a woman, wanting and hungry. Instead of his legacy, he'd shoved his wet cock back into his trousers. He didn't even button up as he stood, offered the young lady his hand, and absconded with her to the nearest open room down the palace hall.

He barely registered the smell of wood shavings and linseed oil—the Royal Woodworker's office—before he tossed her on the velvet settee in front of the fireplace and rucked up her lace skirts.

Alexander had proceeded to fuck her with his tongue until her screams of pleasure were louder than the harps and bloody trumpets. After he'd wrenched her first orgasm out of her, she tugged the chain around her neck until it revealed a locket hidden between her breasts. She opened it to find the dry red-capped mushrooms that prevented their brief, passionate release from conceiving anything other than mutual pleasure.

Being with her had turned out to be a better way to spend the evening. Part of him knew that his duty was in the banquet hall. As the Sword of the Realm, he was the king's shield. But it was a feast day, and besides, Wilhelm had already reminded him of his uselessness. Alexander's position as the Sword of the Realm was as decorative as the glass baubles enchanted to dance along the ceiling. Everyone knew it.

"Your Highness," she screamed. "Yes, please, Your Highness!"

"Sweetheart," he purred. "I am currently inside of you. I believe we can drop the formalities. Call me Alexander."

"*Alexander*," she hollered. She really did have a powerful set of lungs. "Right *there*. Right *there*."

She slapped her palms on his abdominal muscles and hooked one of her legs around his thigh. He matched her rhythm, the way she clawed at his chest and rolled her hips. He sat up and gripped her narrow waist, her generous curves bouncing against him. She was so soft, it was like fucking a cloud, and he'd often wondered what that would feel like, as it was Alexander's goal in life to fuck everyone and everything that would have him.

The Sweet Maiden wiggled and searched for her pleasure, using him, biting at his shoulder, his bottom lip, until she broke around him, hollering her orgasm in waves around his throbbing cock.

When she was ready, she eased herself off his lap, kissing the hard pink flesh coated in her slick orgasm.

"I didn't get to taste you before," she said, crawling to him.

He half growled, half laughed. "So, that's what you're after."

"I've heard rumors about you." Her pale cheeks turned blotchy for a moment.

He took her chin in his fist and brushed her lips with his thumb. His cock gave an agonizing jolt, dripping and needing release.

"Not all rumors are true," he told her, and she frowned.

It was a legend, as so much of his lineage was. The descendants of the first Saint had the power to grant wishes, gifts, tithes of their mortal bodies. Saint Nikolas had orchestrated it that way. He had left his homeland in search of paradise, and he had succeeded. When he created the Eternal Winter Forest, joining his followers with the fae who had lived in the woods for eons, he'd cemented his legacy.

His first child would bear the Mark of the Saint—the magic to heal, be it tree or stone or blood or bone. The magic to be part of the Forest, connected in a way only the true king could. Then there was the second-born—the Master of Alchemy, who would always keep the kingdom in riches. Together, there would be no sickness, no famine, no evil.

Yes, there had been third and fourth children from the royal family, but they were rare. In the event of a spare, like Alexander, they were given honorary positions and the dregs of the magic that flowed through the other heirs. But Alexander had been the very first Sword of the Realm.

Despite his title, the youngest prince's true prowess and unofficial title was Master of Sex. The kingdom needed one, and somewhere among his conquests, his own legend had been born. Unlike his brothers, Alexander's power was baser, primal. He had the power of mirth. Pleasure. Some claimed his seed possessed the ability to cure the deepest melancholy. It was a gift Alexander took seriously. If he could give one thing of himself, then let it be the only body he had. The thing about the powers of the descendants of Saint Nikolas was they manifested in different ways, and the deeper Alexander believed his greatest power was pleasure, the more his body became a well of it. So much so that even his seed became a subject of ardent desire.

"Perhaps this rumor is true," he told his Sweet Maiden.

She brightened at that, licking at his shaft and sucking his tip like a kitten with a fresh bowl of cream. "And it'll taste like anything?"

He rocked his head back and his hips upward. "It'll taste like your heart's content."

"But how?" She silenced her own whine by taking him deeper, faster.

Alexander had no answer. The archivist had no records of his gifts, and his brothers believed his talents were exaggerated, the jealous fucks. So, Alexander simply gave of his body. He gave in the only way he could, as a warrior in a time of eternal peace. He fucked. He licked. He reveled.

Alexander could hear the ringing of bells in the distance, perhaps the end of the feast and beginning of the midnight bacchanals. But he was so close, so close to his release. He squeezed the root of his cock to increase the sensation.

"That's it," he said, panting.

The Sweet Maiden gazed up at him for approval. She swallowed his dick whole, his swollen head grazing the roof of her mouth. He felt her tense, then dig her nails at his hips to keep him in place. She hummed with pleasure, and it vibrated against his sensitive flesh as she pushed herself further, taking him deeper into her throat.

"How terribly naughty you are," he whispered darkly.

And it was there, at the sight of her, that he tipped over the edge. He knew this was the reason why he'd been destined to be the spare. The one who did not neatly fit into his family. Because he'd rather get his cock wet than spend the high festivals watching the kingdom beg for miracles from their cold sainted king.

"I'm going to—" he began to warn.

She moaned and opened up as he came to a delicious peak, heart hammering against his ribs. As a clamor of bells and singing flooded every part of the palace, so did his orgasm. His seed spilled from the corners of her mouth, and she dragged a finger to catch his spend.

She offered a coy smile when she noticed he was propped on his elbows, delighting in the sight of her. "I've never tasted anything like it. Like sweet cream."

Alexander laughed. Sweet cream seemed to be a favorite among his lovers. Though there was one instance when a sailor had favorited the taste of salt.

"Come now," Alexander said, reaching for his trousers. "It sounds like the banquet is over, and I should escort you back in time for dancing."

As they tugged on their clothes and laced up, the doors to the office slammed open. A knight in green ceremonial dress braced himself against the threshold. He hurriedly glanced from the corridor and into the room.

The Sweet Maiden yelped and finished yanking at the laces of her dress.

"We have one rule—" Alexander growled, but the knight's terror-stricken face put a stop to Alexander's threat. "What is it?"

"Lady Arabella, Prince Alexander—" the young man panted. "The king— Your brother—"

"He's not king *yet*." Alexander sighed dismissively. He pulled at the front of his tailcoat. "I don't care what he wants. You of all people know better than to interrupt me, especially at the behest of my brothers. You're *my* knight, sworn to me. Not his—"

"*Dead*," the knight wailed the interruption. "Your brother is dead."

2
LIA

Noelia Espinoza had never done an impulsive thing in her life.

Everything, from her groceries to her five-year plan, was neatly written in her color-coded planner. She even scheduled five minutes on Sunday nights to have a good cry about the things that stressed her out—her father's money-hemorrhaging restaurant, the anxiety of telling her father she did not want to *run* said money-hemorrhaging restaurant, her fizzling relationship, a meme of a cute dog—anything. Five minutes might not seem like a long time to some and too much to others, but it was her five minutes.

So, when George Russo, the boyfriend she'd been working up the courage to break up with, took her to a fancy restaurant and proposed marriage, Lia packed a bag and went as far away as possible.

George was good on paper. He'd been the literal boy next door and her first kiss. First heartbreak, too, when he'd left to boarding school in England for high school. He was the stuff of teenage dreams.

When he'd returned home almost seventeen years later to

take care of his aging mother, Lia was surprised that all those childhood feelings had returned with a vengeance.

At thirty-four, George was extremely successful, family oriented, and had an actual savings account. At thirty-three, Lia was stuck working publicity for the family restaurant, couldn't stand up to her parents, and despite her best attempts, she'd never been in love.

When he'd asked her out for brunch, they played "Where Are They Now?" with everyone they knew. At first it was sweet. They held hands. They kissed goodnight. He always offered to pay for the check, even though she insisted on splitting most times. Their families liked each other. He took her to work functions and bought her lavish gifts.

But then she started noticing little things. On their dates, George never looked into her eyes for long, and she'd caught him checking out waitresses on more than one occasion. He did seventy percent of the talking, usually about finance and investments. When she expressed her opinion on anything—from pizza toppings to the news—he always made a huge show as to why she was wrong. When she chose one of her own dresses to a work function instead of one he'd picked out, he'd be passive aggressive all evening.

He'd even laughed when she'd mentioned, during their third date, that she was still a virgin. Most people laughed, simply because they thought she was joking. She'd learned to brush off comments because it wasn't something Lia was embarrassed about. It simply hadn't happened. There were two moments, during her first kiss with George when they were kids, and on their first date, that she thought it might have been him one day. But then she got to know him, and the cracks in his ultra-polished veneer started to show.

Lia was notoriously bad at standing up for herself, and it had taken her three months to work up the courage to break things off. Instead, George has proposed. And after choking on a spoonful of raspberry cheesecake, the clearest choice had been to flee.

The only hitch in her plan was that her sisters had decided, no—insisted—on coming along.

"We're here when you're ready to talk," Helena said on the drive to the airport. As the eldest of the Espinoza sisters, Helena was fiercely protective of Lia and Gracie. She'd do anything for them, even if it meant trekking to the other side of the world a week before Christmas.

But Lia hadn't been ready to talk. Not during the long flight, with her sisters using her as a human pillow. Not when they picked up the rental car and Lia concentrated on driving with a German GPS that sounded angry as it led them to their bed and breakfast.

Baden-Baden, Germany was quiet, right out of a Grimm's fairytale, with gingerbread houses and a countryside blanketed in snow and patches of forest. Their bed and breakfast was a tiny house that looked like a cuckoo clock on the outside but was modern on the inside.

While her sisters unpacked, Lia turned on her phone and watched the messages light up like the tree at Rockefeller Center. Her mother was worried. Her father was disappointed. George was patient, if irked.

Lia hadn't brought much with her. A carry-on containing a couple of pairs of pants, three merino wool sweaters, underthings, toiletries, and her passport. She wore the waterproof jacket she'd bought three years ago for a ski trip during which she did no skiing. But the most important thing she carried in her worn leather satchel was her planner and bag of journaling supplies.

She carried it from her cozy bedroom to the cozier kitchen table. She flipped through a year's worth of to-do lists. Neat, curved handwriting in blue, purple, pink, green. All the way at the very back was her five-year plan:

Finish my novel
Buy an apartment
Get driver's license
Go on a vacation
Fall madly in love
Get married
Help my parents retire

At some point, her sisters had walked up beside her and started reading over her shoulder.

"*Hmm*. Does this count as a vacation?" Gracie asked in her upbeat voice. She didn't even look as jetlagged as Lia felt.

"You went to Niagara Falls over the summer," Helena chimed in. "That definitely counts as a vacation."

Helena reached for a green gel pen, but Lia snatched it away before her sister could check it off.

Lia shut the notebook and retracted the pen tip. "You guys know I mean a fancy vacation in Bali where I have my own house and an infinity pool with floating trays of sushi for lunch."

Helena and Gracie exchanged a look, one that told Lia she was being unreasonable. The three of them shared the same burnt umber brown eyes, bushy eyebrows, and jet-black hair. Helena took after their tall mother, with a sharp jaw, sharper tongue, and light brown skin dusted in freckles. Gracie and Lia were more like their father, average height, and honey tan skin that was always gold in the summer. Lia, however, had been the only one to inherit both their parents' worries and anxieties.

The three of them were a team, and she realized how incredibly blessed she was to have them with her.

"All, right," Helena said, opening up cabinets until she found a bottle of wine that had dust on it. "We're doing this."

Gracie pressed her lips together and shook her head. "I don't think Lia should drink and make a huge decision."

"I'm not making a decision this minute," Lia said.

Helena ignored their youngest sister and emptied the entire bottle into three glasses. They couldn't properly *cheers* out of fear they'd slosh the burgundy liquid everywhere.

"Start at the beginning," Gracie said. "I thought you were breaking up."

"So did I," Lia said, rubbing the side of her temple. "For weeks he'd been curt and only responded in one-word texts and thumbs up emojis. We were running on fumes. Or so I thought."

Helena pursed her lips. She was not a fan of George. "Maybe he didn't notice you've been upset, since he can't actually tell the difference between his ass and his elbow."

"That's not constructive." Gracie elbowed Helena before turning her attention back to Lia. "How did he propose?"

Lia had imagined her marriage proposal since she'd had a Zac Efron poster taped to her bedroom wall all through high school. She'd always been the most romantic of her sisters, and usually kept those things to herself and the pages of her journals. One of the most elaborate scenarios had been that Zac would take her to a Broadway musical then get called on stage for an impromptu cameo. Then, he'd get down on one knee and look up at their seat, in the balcony of course, and he'd say, "Noelia Espinoza, would you do me the honor of being my one true forever love?"

The way it had actually happened was, George had changed the dinner location she'd picked. Lia avoided the way her sisters cringed.

"We usually go to gastropubs and casual restaurants," she

said, "and I read breakups are better in public places. Plus, this way it was in my budget when I insisted on picking up the check."

"Yeah, they say that so there are witnesses," Helena muttered.

"So, we end up at his favorite steak house," Lia continues. "I was just getting to it during desert, when he cleared his throat and said, 'Lia, we've been friends a long time. You're practical, smart, loyal. You're not shallow and dramatic like other women. These past few months have made me realize that you and I would make a good match. We're not getting any younger, and I think we're both ready to settle down.'"

Gracie made a "yikes" face. "How romantic."

"*Then*, he opened a little blue velvet box and slid it across the table, like he was slipping me a *business* proposal. That's when I started choking, and he rushed to say, 'Don't worry, I've spoken with your father. He's given his blessing!'"

"Dad must've eaten that shit up," Gracie said.

Lia frowned. She'd had the same frown since she was the most serious, orderly little girl in kindergarten. Only instead of being mad when her books weren't alphabetized, she was frustrated and furious that the biggest decision of her life had been machinated without her.

"Well," Helena said, glancing between her sisters. "Where's the ring?"

Lia rolled her eyes. "*That's* your takeaway?"

"What our Hell Belle means is," Gracie said, always the peacekeeper, "it's a big part of the story, and we would, you know, like to see it."

Lia snatched up her backpack. The ring was in one of the many waterproof pockets beside her passport, keys, and emergency protein bars she kept during her commute to work. She fished it out and set it at the center of the table. It was a pear-shaped diamond in a gold setting.

"It doesn't even fit," Lia said, shoving the ring as far as it would go on her finger.

Helena snorted. "You sweet summer child."

"I'm not naïve." But even as she said it, Lia didn't believe herself.

"No, but you're a hopeless romantic," Helena said, her voice gentler than when she talked about George. "He's shown you exactly who he is from the beginning, but you've been in love with the cute little boy who lived next door. You're so in love with love you stay even when the relationship flat lines."

Lia nodded and tugged on the ring to loosen it. "I know. I know... I just keep thinking about the things he liked about me—practical, smart, loyal. Without the practical part he might as well have been listing qualities in a dog."

"I also did not like his comment about *other women*," Gracie intoned.

"Don't get mad at me, but," Helena said, "why didn't you say no? Why come here instead?"

That was the million-dollar question Lia had been asking herself for the last twenty-four hours. An uneasy sensation wedged itself in her throat, filled with all her insecurities and every ugly feeling that had plagued her for years. That she was unlovable. That she was too odd to desire. Not beautiful enough to evoke passion. That her dreams were just that—dreams. That perhaps an arrangement, an understanding, no matter how loveless and passionless, was better than nothing.

Staring at the two people she couldn't lie to, Lia swallowed the emotional pill and said the most honest thing she could. "What if this is my only chance?"

"Oh, babe. You're not a cow being put out to pasture," Gracie told her.

"Need I remind you that I'm older than you by three years," Helena said, wrapping an arm around her younger sister. "And I'm perfectly happy being single?"

"Yes, but you've also never been a thirty-three-year-old virgin who has never had a serious long-term relationship," Lia said.

Gracie snorted. "Technically, George might be it."

Lia fished out her emergency protein bar, but Helena smacked it out of her hand.

"We did not fly across the globe to eat cardboard." Helena grimaced. "We're going out."

"Where? The Black Forest night club?" Gracie asked.

"No, smartass," Helena said.

"I'm hungry now," Lia grumbled.

Helena made quick work of pulling up a map on her phone. "I Googled what the fuck there was to do around here and there's a Christmas market nearby. We're going to fill up on carbs and sausages and something called *glühwein*. I love you so much that I'll be the designated driver."

Lia took a steadying breath and grinned at her sisters. It dawned on her that they'd dropped everything they were doing —Helena at her law firm and Gracie at the hospital—and come with her. She felt silly for having reacted so out of character. So *impractical*. Perhaps she'd done that as her own rebellion against George's judgement. Perhaps she'd wanted to prove something, not to him, but to herself. No matter the reason, at least she wasn't alone, and she couldn't let the time they had go to waste. Besides, she'd read somewhere that she needed to force her body to stay awake, otherwise she'd never get acclimated to the new time zone.

So, the Espinoza sisters made the short drive to the Christmas market where neat rows of wooden stalls spread out in all directions. Tourists and locals migrated from food vendors to artisanal trinkets. Lia bought a funny little Santa Claus ornament with pink cheeks that reminded her Christmas was her *actual* favorite holiday. She also bought an eggnog-colored wool hat and scarf since she'd forgotten those things in her rush to get to the airport.

In the early afternoon, the sun shone behind a thick cover of clouds. Lia filled her belly with buttery pretzels, melted cheese, and hot *glühwein*.

Even though she promised herself she wouldn't, she looked at her phone. George had texted.

It read: Lia. Can we talk?

While her sisters gathered for some sort of pageant where a little girl in a gold wig and dress brought out presents for children, Lia walked away from the crowds and toward the line of decorated trees. Her entire body was hot with nerves and mulled wine. She unzipped her coat and shoved her wool beanie into her backpack.

Helena and Gracie would tell her to ignore the phone, but she needed to settle this.

She hit the call button, and the hot flash settled into her as she walked up the marked trail decorated with giant candy canes.

"Hey," George said, friendly even.

"Hi," she said.

"I understand my proposal might have been a bit of a shock," he said. "Though I didn't expect you to react so viscerally that you needed to go to Germany."

"I was definitely shocked and needed to think. Maybe we aren't on the same page."

She could practically hear him shrug. "Feels like a no-brainer. We match, don't we, Lia? And our families have been friends for ages. I know you said you haven't had a long-term relationship before, and assumed you weren't one of those women who needed all of that fake romance stuff."

Again, *those women*. She hated that he said it that way. Well, what if she was *one of those women*? What if she wanted romance stuff? Why were people determined to put those things down like they didn't matter? Was it too much to *want* to be wanted? Was it too much to want love?

"I need you to answer one thing." Her throat was dry, but she swallowed and spoke. "Do you love me?"

Did she want the answer to be yes? Would that make her choice easier? Would that change her mind?

George sighed. "I thought we were both more practical than that. When I spoke to your father—"

"What century are you living in?" She hadn't meant to raise her voice, but the wind was picking up, and she had to shout. "You should have talked to *me*. You should have asked *me*."

"You're right." He sounded eager to correct his mistake. "You have to admit that you're considering it. Deep down, I know that we want the same things. Partnership. Family. Would it be so bad, Lia? Come home and we can talk like adults. You're acting as bratty as Helena."

"I've asked you not to talk about my sister that way," she said, her voice tight with emotion.

She stopped walking, and when she closed her eyes to the sky, she felt the gentle press of snowflakes on her eyelids.

No, she didn't need more time to think. She wanted true love. George wasn't it. Sure, relationships weren't easy. She never asked for easy. But they weren't whatever they had either. Anger and sadness ripped through her. But something else. Strength, too. Strength that had only come from her sisters. She spoke the words she couldn't the day before.

"Look, George. I can't do this."

"Are you seriously breaking up with me over the phone?"

"I'm sorry. I should have said something yesterday. We don't want the same things. I'll give you the ring back as soon as I get home."

He scoffed. "No one would give you the life I can."

"Goodbye, George."

"You'll—"

His voice came in garbled before the call dropped. She stared at her phone and saw that she had no service bars. You'll what? Regret it? Then how come she'd never felt lighter? She turned around to walk back the way she came from, following the trail marked by candy canes.

Only when she stepped in a circle, there were no candy canes around at all. She was in a thicket of naked trees and snow.

"Okay. Okay. Okay. At least the sun's still out," she muttered out loud. "I can navigate."

Who was she kidding? Born and raised in New York City, she had muscle memory for one thing: the subway.

She pulled up the map app. She'd downloaded offline maps during their wait at the airport. But when she zoomed in, the map didn't orient itself, and the tiny blue dot that marked her location was frozen.

"Shit!" Panic kickstarted her heart like a bass drum. "I definitely went in a straight line."

Had she? She was jet lagged and buzzed and hadn't been paying as much attention as she should have. She began to walk back. The call had barely been ten minutes. But when she went back the way she came, she didn't see the market. Couldn't even hear bells and music. She turned around and prayed to every deity in the world that she was on one of those loop trails that end up where they started.

Instead, she arrived at a fork in the road.

"Nice." One path was shadowed with felled trees. The

other side was pristine, clear. Neat and uncomplicated as George was supposed to be. "Good going, Universe."

She tried her phone again, but the app crashed. Snow melted on its screen, and she decided to stow it in her waterproof pocket. It only made sense that the trail was a loop, and it had to be the plowed path. Yes, that would lead her back to the market.

She shoved her hands in her pockets and went full steam ahead. She was not about to wind up frozen in some German forest. Helena and Gracie were either calling the American embassy or still shoving their faces full of grilled sausages.

At the thought of her sisters, she walked faster, boots leaving deep prints in the snow. There definitely had not been that much snow when she'd turned into the candy cane forest, and she had the terrifying thought that the forest was going to swallow her whole.

It was then that the sky ripped open, and sleet pelted at her. Cold seeped through her high-tech winter gear, and gusts of icy wind threatened to push her off her feet. Panic dug its claws into her. Everywhere she turned, there was nothing but snow, nothing but spindly branches slapping against the gale. There wasn't even a path she could take.

This wasn't happening. This *couldn't* happen. This hadn't been on her list.

"Help!" she screamed.

Lia Espinoza was hopelessly, regrettably lost. And there was no one to hear her beneath the howling wind.

3
ALEXANDER

His brother wasn't dead. Couldn't be dead.

But as the banquet revelers flooded the corridor, their terrified cries echoing through the high ceilings, Alexander's reality came crashing down. A hot, sickening sensation tore through him because if he could trust anything in the palace, it was the knight sworn to him since childhood.

"Get her to safety," Alexander commanded.

"I must—"

Alexander clutched his friend's shoulder. "I know your vow. Go. *Now*."

If there had been time, Alexander would have kissed her hand, assured her that everything would be all right. That the commotion was a misunderstanding. After all, nothing like this was supposed to happen in the Eternal Winter Forest, their paradise away from the wretchedness of the human world.

Alexander had to see for himself. He unsheathed his sword and made for the banquet hall. The swell of people felt like swimming against a rushing current. He searched the crowd for injuries, but the small relief was that no one was hurt as far as he could see.

Terror was not a feeling he was accustomed to. Not since—

He wrenched away from those old memories and tore open the double doors. Hadn't he just been there, bickering with his brothers? Hadn't he just wished he could be anywhere but these festivities?

There, in the banquet hall, the screams were distant. He tasted bile. His leather boots crushed glass with every step. Wine ran from upturned goblets. Chairs lay on their backs, and he could almost see the moment everyone stood abruptly and ran, leaving behind the feast that now littered the marble floor. He could hear his own heartbeat slamming in his ears, his vision blurred at the edges.

"Will?" Alexander never used his brother's diminutive. The last time had been when they were boys. Before their father had shoved Alexander to the side and reminded Wilhelm and Hans that they were the true heirs of their blessed legacy. Before they had started turning into people he couldn't stand to be beside.

But he repeated the name because it was all he could summon. "Will?"

Alexander rounded the table and saw his brother. He lay in a pool of blood and blue silk. A fine red line trickled from the corner of his open mouth. His bejeweled hand was fisted over his heart, where blood flowed fresh and fast.

"Fuck," Alexander gritted between clenched teeth. He clapped his hand over his brother's to stop the blood.

Will made a pained, gurgling sound, then coughed up blood. He grabbed Alexander by the collar and pulled him down. There had been a time when Alexander had been small and easy to kick and shove like a runt. There had been a time when Wilhelm was stronger. But his grip was weak and fading.

"Fuck. You bloody fool." Alexander exhaled a sob. "Heal yourself, dammit! You are the Nikolas!"

A pained smile tugged at his brother's face. He managed to say a single word. "No."

"What do you mean no?" It was then that Alexander took a better look at his brother. The Mark of the Saint was fading from his skin. The black ink, once in the body, only disappeared when the Nikolas died.

Alexander looked around helplessly. Where was Celeste? Where was Hans? Where were the bloody guards?

Where had Alexander, the Sword of the Realm, been when his brother was murdered?

"Brother—" Wilhelm said once, then sighed his final breath. Sharp amber eyes glistened with tears that ran down the sides of his face and stared, lifeless, at the blazing lights on the ceiling.

Alexander rested his forehead against his brother's, then closed Wilhelm's eyelids.

"Blessed are the dead for they know no pain at journey's end."

The saying was hollow, meaningless because Wilhelm had felt pain.

"Alexander!"

Alexander shot up and drew his sword. Hans raised his palms, the edge of the blade digging just enough to slick a single cut across the golden prince's skin.

"*Who* did this?" Alexander asked, taking a step back but keeping his blade drawn and steady.

"Easy, Alexander," Hans said, panting. He rubbed at a stain on his suit and scoffed. "I've risked my very precious ass to come back for you. Celeste has bewitched the guard."

"Celeste?"

Hans knelt to their brother's side. His face was unmoving as the golden statue he resembled. But for a moment, he pressed his forehead to their dead brother and whispered the same final words Alexander had moments before.

The moment did not last.

Hans, despite being the shortest of the three, shoved Alexander to the back of the banquet hall, behind the great pine tree dripping with glass decorations and candles. There, he touched his finger to a sconce, and a narrow panel opened.

"Please, brother. Don't argue," Hans said.

Hans had never uttered the word *please*. Not to Alexander and likely not to anyone else. But more than that, there was something Alexander had never heard in his brother's voice before—fear.

Alexander cast a final glance at the ruined feast and took the secret path through the palace. He inhaled the cool scent of wet stone. Bits of phosphorescent crystals were embedded in the gray walls, an invention from a Master of Alchemy two centuries before. The last time the kingdom had erupted into violence, and the same time the queen had tunnels built within the palace to help the royal family escape.

The steady pounding of their boots and the relentless speed of his heart was all Alexander could hear. It drove him mad.

"Why would Celeste kill her own husband?" Alexander asked.

Hans glanced back with a dark look. "How should I know why she does what she does?"

"For once in your life, answer a bloody question directly, Hansel."

"I don't know why Celeste has betrayed us!" His words mingled with irritation and disgust. "But one moment I was opening a bottle of the reserve bubbly, to toast to *her*. Because Wilhelm wanted to toast his bloody future queen. Then next moment she's got a blade in her hand. She conjured the bloody thing from the ether like she was one of the Helleböorne Priestesses."

Alexander had seen the priestesses at work. They prayed to

the moon and practiced nature sex magic. They didn't gut people, especially not the future king. "Where is she now?"

Hans shook his head. "That's the part that worries me. She—"

"That's the part? Not our dead brother choking on his own blood?"

"Even now you are an insufferable twat," Hans said in his crisp, malevolently cheerful tone. "It worries me that she dispersed the royal guard. Half of them were corralling people back into the village."

Alexander had a bad feeling about what would come next. "And the other half?"

"They're after you."

"Not you?"

Hans made a sharp right into a dead end. Alexander recognized the soft scent of freshly baked bread. They opened the hatch and crawled out of a door small enough to let in a hound. The kitchens were abandoned. A fire blazed in the hearth, and trays of food were laid out, never to be served to the promised king.

Hans ripped out a piece of meat from a roasted pork shoulder and ate it, then dusted his hands. "Don't look at me like that."

"Why is Celeste looking for me, Hansel?" Alexander asked, exasperated.

"Isn't it obvious?" Hans filled a copper cup with wine. Alexander's stomach turned. How could he think of eating and drinking when their brother was dead? Murdered. "You're next in line to inherit the Mark of the Saint."

Alexander shook his head. "You're the second-born."

Hans smiled darkly. "And I was born with my pretty shackles, brother." He held up his arm, displaying the golden runes on his inner wrist.

But Alexander wouldn't hear of it. "No. Absolutely not."

Suddenly, the kitchen, despite its open wooden ceiling and arched windows displaying the early evening sky, was suffocating. Alexander was not born to be the king of the Eternal Winter Forest. Blood pounding in his ears, he was half aware of Hans explaining the edict their family legacy was rooted in—Saint Nikolas had imbued his first two sons with magical gifts, and they passed them down for decades, for *centuries*. There was never a need to worry about what would happen because the royals lived out the full extent of their mortal lives. Because the Eternal Winter Kingdom was paradise.

His father had never so much as had a cold because it was impossible.

It was impossible that Alexander should have to be king when he'd spent thirty-five years of his life understanding that his very being was a useless, wasteful mistake. All he'd ever done was embarrass his family. All he'd ever done was fuck his way through the land. All he was *supposed* to do was stand by his brother, at the king's side, and protect him. And he'd even failed to do that.

"No—"

Hans licked wine from his lower lip. A riot of emotion cycled through his features—anger, frustration, and then the realization that he would get nowhere with Alexander if he yelled. "Brother. Please. I *won't* hear of it. You're going to accept the Mark of the Saint, and you're going to stand in the bloody place of kings and become the next King Nikolas. I know you hate this family, but the kingdom needs a Nikolas."

Alexander sneered. Yes, most days he hated his brothers. But he didn't want them dead. He wanted them to be better than their cold, cruel father. He wanted them to keep the promises they made to the people. He wanted them to be worthy of the legacy they were born into. Even when he hated them, he wanted to love them because they were his blood, and if they were wretched, then it meant that he had no choice but to be wretched, too.

"The kingdom needs a leader, not a Nikolas," Alexander said in a rush. He thought he might shake apart from his racing heart. "If Celeste wants me for the Mark of the Saint, then I simply won't let it take root."

"Alexander—" Hans looked to the door behind them. The door that led to the courtyard and had a direct path to the stables. "There has always been and will always be a Nikolas. You must claim the Mark by tomorrow's solstice, or it will *end* the line. You're mourning, we both are, but you're not seeing things clearly."

"I am, Hansel. And I know that you can rule our people without the bloody mark of a saint who's been dead for eons." Alexander drew his sword and backed away to the door.

Hans threw his glass, and Alexander sliced through it. "Alexander! Don't you fucking dare."

But Alexander knocked over a tray, gravy and mash slathering Hans's clothes. The diversion would not last, and he slid out the door, barricading it with a barrel.

"Kilian!" Alexander shouted as he ran toward the stables. He hoped and prayed that his loyal friend would be able to hear him. He tugged at the chain in his pocket and withdrew a whistle, light as air, and blew. The runes etched in the metal illuminated with its enchantment. Only Kilian and Alexander could hear its piercing cry.

As a line of guards spilled into the courtyard, he heard his name on their lips. Alexander crouched low behind a hedge. The horses kicked and whinnied. Alexander blew the whistle once more. When he pocketed the trinket, he noticed that his hands were covered in his brother's blood. He dug his fists into the snow and scraped at it, but it wouldn't come off.

It was then that he heard the thundering sound of hooves. A russet reindeer hurled its way toward him. He swung his horns and barreled through the guards, trotting to a stop.

"Kilian," Alexander said, almost breathless with relief.

The creature huffed and bobbed its head. Alexander shoved his boot in the stirrup and hoisted himself onto the saddle. Kilian took off the moment Alexander had hold of the reins. He glanced back. The guards were recovering. Bells rang from the cathedral.

Alexander forced himself to look straight ahead as they cut through the village square. Like the banquet hall, Solaris Square looked abruptly abandoned. Doors and windows were shut, and a few guards tried to give chase. But no one was faster than Kilian was.

Alexander welcomed the cold slap of the wind as they raced across the frozen salt flats and the path that cut through the Týrin Valley, all the way through the Elfenhörn Forest.

Kilian bucked as they approached the tree line. They both knew no one was supposed to enter the forest, by decree of the old royals.

"The king is dead," Alexander said, and kicked his reindeer's flanks.

As the sun began to set, Kilian stomped through the forbidden forest. There was only one place far enough Alexander could go to escape his family and wait out the solstice.

The human realm.

The forest was eerily silent. Alexander wondered if the old spirits could feel his brother's passing in the ancient magic that had connected each Nikolas to the land. He tucked his head between his shoulders but couldn't avoid every branch that tore at his tailcoat or nicked his cheek. He'd only ever strayed in this forest once, and he'd sworn to never return.

He'd also sworn to protect his brother, and so it seemed like a day made for broken promises.

Alexander felt the change in the forest, the pressure that hummed as they approached the border between their realm and the other. His ears popped, and his guts were gripped by a vise-like sensation. He couldn't breathe for a moment, a moment that stretched as Kilian sprang over an ancient fallen tree and landed in a prism of blue light and snow. Not just the delicate flurries that sifted through the sky during winter, coating the Eternal Winter Kingdom in velvety white. This was a howling storm, twisting and turning them in a circle.

Somehow, he heard it.

Heard her.

"Please. Help me!" A voice full of the same terror pumping in his veins.

Alexander blinked at the snowflakes that obscured his vision. He caught her waving arms, her face obscured by the hood of her overcoat. She was struggling to dig herself out of a snowbank in a clearing.

He nudged Kilian forward. He reached for her, but then she reeled away from him, falling hard on her back.

Perplexed, Alexander looked down at what could have caused that reaction. Then he noticed the blood caked under his nails, his rugged state from the run through the forest.

"I'm trying to save you!" he shouted, dismounting in a fluid sweep of his leg.

As she scrambled on her back to right herself, Alexander felt the ground *move*. He looked down, too late, to notice they were on a slab of ice. A frozen lake. Kilian's hooves stomped, trying to retreat, and it only worsened the vibration that rippled beneath their feet.

"Stop! Do *not* move!" Alexander shouted, keeping a foot on firm ground.

Her hood fell back. Her eyes were shut. Tears had turned to ice on her cheek bones. Her breath came in puffs of condensation snatched up by the harsh wind. He couldn't hear her, but he knew the word she was whimpering, to him, or herself, or a merciless god.

"Please."

"Get on your belly," he said, his deep voice firm and clear. "Crawl to me. I won't hurt you."

He wished that she'd open her eyes. That perhaps she'd see in his face that he meant every word. But as she got to her stomach, there was a deep, resounding *crack*.

The lake broke open and swallowed her beneath its icy waters.

4
ALEXANDER

Alexander needed to keep running. It was why he'd turned his back on everything he knew and left.

But as he watched the strange woman fall through the ice, he remembered the sound he'd managed to hear beneath the gale of the snowstorm.

Please, she'd said. Begged.

The supplication broke something inside of him. He'd failed to protect the future king, and he'd failed to take up the legacy left behind. This, this he could do.

"Kilian, stay back. If you fall through, then I fear we're all lost."

The reindeer snuffed in response.

The last time Alexander had stripped naked that quickly, it had been during the Mistletoe Moon Festival, and he'd stumbled upon an orgy.

Now, he tossed his clothes over his saddle. The ice on his skin had no effect, thanks to the fae blood of his early ancestors. Though as he walked to the break in the ice, he knew no fae or saintly inheritance could give him the ability to breathe underwater. He had to find her, and fast.

THE HEART OF WINTER

Alexander dove into the frigid dark.

At first, it was like being submerged in bathwater. He swam in a circle. Tiny bubbles escaped from his nose. The water was so unpolluted, it was like she was floating in air. Seconds stretched into small eternities as his chest began to feel uncomfortable. His lungs wanted to contract and get fresh air. But he held his breath and swam until he spotted her.

Alexander swam hard, never taking his eyes off her. The closer he got, the more he had the urge to suck in a breath, because her beauty was like a kick to his solar plexus. High cheekbones, darkest lashes. Her raven hair billowed like spilled ink. Full lips that were bright pink, edging on purple. A bruise bloomed on her forehead, contracting against her golden tan skin.

Open your eyes, he thought.

He *needed* to see her open her eyes. To know she wasn't dead, but unconscious.

Finally, he reached her. His arms and legs hurt to move, the cold beginning to stiffen his muscles. He wrapped an arm around her and swam upward. There was no time to find the other entry point, and he was losing the air trapped in his aching lungs.

He balled his hand into a fist and punched the sheet of ice above. Again. And again. And once more. Light leeched from his sight for a moment, but he held on tightly to her. He had to save her. There was no sinking, no drowning, no freezing to death. He pulled his arm back and felt the rush of fire in his veins, redoubling his strength until his numb fist broke the ice.

Slabs of snowy lake splashed into the water as he smashed through the surface and took a painful breath. He gripped the ledge with bloody fingers and pushed her up and over. He prayed that the surface would hold. Then, Alexander hauled himself out. He had a sliver of a moment to lay on his back. Hail pelted his face and wet, naked body. The warm blood that spilled from his torn knuckles was a shock to his system.

Please. He heard her voice again, sharp and clear, as if she was awake right beside him.

Alexander had not left his kingdom only to drown in the human realm. He propped himself up on his side and dragged them both, burning and scraping every inch of him, until he reached Kilian.

The reindeer bit the girl's sleeve and dragged her to safe ground while Alexander staggered to his feet. In seconds, the remainder of the lake shattered and broke off into pieces as trees fell into it.

Alexander went to the woman's side. He touched the pulse point at her throat. It was slow but strong. He let out a sigh of relief that surprised him. He'd felt more relief knowing she, this utter stranger, was alive than when he'd seen Hans, his own flesh and blood.

Pushing the sentiment away, he cupped the back of her neck and breathed into her. Kilian nudged his shoulder, and Alexander swatted his wet snout away.

"I bloody *know* that," Alexander answered, unzipping her strange coat and stacked his palms against her chest. The first thing he'd learned when he trained with the guard was field trauma. He'd paid attention because even if he'd never expected a war to fight in, people could still drown.

He counted each pump, then breathed into her mouth. She was so cold. So cold. He couldn't let her die. He didn't understand the frenzied need he had to make sure she took another breath. All he knew was that he had to see her open her eyes. She simply had to.

The first moment she began retching lake water from her lungs was the moment Alexander turned his head back to the unrelenting storm and thanked the saint.

THE HEART OF WINTER

With no signs of the snow stopping, Alexander didn't bother to dress. He draped the half-conscious girl across the saddle and grabbed Kilian by the reigns, trudging through the snow as fast as they could.

There was only one place where they could go in such a blizzard. They were close enough to the border between the realms. *Too* close to home, but his only other choice was letting the woman he'd saved from drowning *freeze* to death while he meandered, lost in a human forest.

The cabin was blanketed in white, but as he approached, the sigil emblazoned on the door flashed like a struck match. Its magic recognized the presence of someone from the Eternal Winter Kingdom, and the green door swung open, letting the cold into the dark threshold.

Alexander scooped up the girl and his frozen clothes in his arms and rushed inside. The massive fireplace contained nothing but cinders. He knew that the central hearth heated the entire cabin, but the guardian hadn't replenished the stack of logs. Alexander carefully draped the girl on the plush settee, then stacked the last three logs in the mouth of the fireplace. He grabbed the matchbox from the mantel.

"You have got to be kidding me, Elowen," Alexander growled as he found a single match. But when he struck it, the thing was dead and wouldn't spark. He was too wet. Snow melted down his naked body. He threw the empty box in the fireplace and cursed this realm and the next.

Alexander got on his knees before the girl. He put his fingers to her throat and felt the faint pulse there, saw her shallow breath. Her lips were more purple than before, and there was a sickly pallor to her burnished golden skin.

He went to rummage through a closet and found a thick fur blanket. He stripped her wet coat and clothes off, then covered her with the bear skin.

"Come on, darling," he whispered.

Alexander knew she needed real warmth. Her body began to tremble. He'd read about how frail human bodies could perish under extreme temperatures, but he'd never seen it outside of the medicine tomes in the palace library. Her pallor and her ragged, shallow breaths were too much for him to bear. She was fighting to live, but she needed heat.

There was only one thing he could do.

He shut his eyes and bit down on the bile that rose to his throat. He was a descendant of Saint Nikolas the Wondrous. A man of miracles. A man of pure goodness. A man who longed for paradise, and his sheer will had made it so. For so long, Alexander had hated the legends of his forefather, but he couldn't deny what was in his blood, etched like runes into his mortal bones.

You are the next Nikolas, Hans had said.

Alexander let the ancient power flood him. The power he'd run away from but now needed more than ever. The first sparks of it were like sunlight warming his eyelids. The chime of magic filled his ears. Its caress ran across every inch of his naked body, gathering across his torso and down his arms until it pooled in his palms.

He exposed the top of her chest and rested his palm there. Gold light pulsed along with his strong heartbeat, spilling in threads into her skin. The magic connected them. He caught glimpses of her life. He saw two women who looked like her. Their smiling faces flooded every memory like a kaleidoscope.

There was no sound, but he knew there was laughter. He felt the love between them. The love she gave willingly. He felt the tug of her desire for—what? For more. For everything. He saw her writing a list of wishes. Her words careful but strong, like every curl was claiming its fate by simply being written.

Who was this girl of wishes and joy? Who was she, and how had she stumbled into his path?

When she stirred, Alexander lifted his hand and broke their connection. Her lips had regained their blush pink, and her eyelids fluttered, but she did not wake.

"Sleep, sunshine," he whispered.

Emotion clamored in his heart. Relief that she was alive. Curiosity about what had brought her here. Anxiety that he'd done everything, and he'd still failed to rouse her. Anger at himself because he'd used the greatest power of Saint Nikolas—resurrection. It had been his ancestor's greatest gift, and it had been outlawed by past kings. This woman hadn't been dead, merely on the brink of it. And yet, he'd summoned it, and the power had come. What right did he have to the legacy he'd abandoned?

And why? Why should he be relieved? He didn't know her, not truly. She was a fool lost in a snowstorm. She'd interrupted his plan to go. Away. Far away.

For a moment, he considered leaving. She'd survive the storm. But one glance at her, peaceful, innocent, and his wretched heart revolted at the idea.

He turned his attention to the fireplace. He called on his magic once again. He summoned a spark. It was all he needed. He blew it from the palm of his hand and into the fireplace, where it roared to life.

They'd need more firewood. They'd need water and food. All of that would come later.

First, he had one final thing to do before he allowed himself a moment of rest.

Alexander walked outside. He squinted against the falling snow and found Kilian around back in the single-stall stable where the guardian's horse usually slept. The reindeer clopped to his hooves, alert.

Alexander buried his face in the creature's side. He secured the saddle and left his sword in its sheath. He wouldn't need it anymore.

"Kilian," he said. A shudder passed through him, but he pushed back the emotion that wanted to clamor to the surface. He wasn't ready. "I release you of your vow, old friend. You can go home."

The reindeer followed him, but Alexander locked the door of the cabin and pressed his body against it. He ran a palm over his hair. He needed to rest.

But then he saw it.

A bruise at the center of his palm.

No, not a bruise.

Inky threads. The coil of a vine. He rubbed at it, as if he expected it to brush away like soot.

The Mark of the Saint had taken root.

5
LIA

Lia dreamt about being rescued by a winter god. He'd slipped out of thin air, surrounded by electric blue light, and come to save her from the freak snowstorm.

So when she opened her bleary eyes and saw a naked man standing in front of the fireplace, Lia was still sure she was dreaming. Or dead. Was there a circle of hell for idiots who got lost in the woods?

Her body ached too much for her to think she was anything but alive. And yet, there was indeed a naked man in front of the fireplace. Even though she couldn't see his face, and he had considerably fewer clothes on than before, she was certain.

It was *him*. The winter god.

She was so grateful to be alive that it took her a moment to realize she was in damp underwear and buried under soft furs. A shiver ran through her, and she wasn't sure if it was because of a draft or the perfect view of his muscular ass.

The ass in question was truly spectacular, the actual definition of a peach ripe waiting for her to take a bite out of it. His legs were thick and strong, dusted with black hair. A bright pain bloomed at the side of her head. She remembered that she'd fallen. *Through* a lake. She remembered recoiling from him because there was blood on his hands, on his cheek. But even still, he'd gone beneath the ice to get her.

Perhaps that was why she wasn't afraid, despite being so vulnerable in nothing but her cotton panties and bralette. The feeling of safety betrayed her New York sensibilities, street smarts, and the imagined conversations she'd have with her sisters. Somehow, she had never felt safer, warmer, like there was sunlight under her skin even though she was in the middle of West Bumble Fuck, Germany.

She peeled off her underwear, hating the damp sensation on her warm skin, and curled into a tight ball. She'd only meant to close her eyes for a moment. To let the headache fade. But when she woke up, her mouth tasted terrible, and her muscles were tight all over. She poked her head out of the covers.

No winter god.

Her momentary disappointment was dispelled when she took in her surroundings. The head of a ferocious polar bear was affixed to the wall over the fireplace. It was startling but regal somehow. Pine garlands lined the exposed beams of the ceiling, and literal boughs of holly decorated the wooden railing that led up to what looked like a loft. A pine tree stood at one end of the cozy living room, but it was devoid of any ornaments. None of the shimmering glitter and tinsel her mother loved to cover every inch of the house with. It was a very rustic Christmas, though it smelled incredible.

Taper candles nearly burned to the stub were nestled into pewter candle holders on the table in front of her. Melted rivers of wax were dried on the surface. The single window was shuttered, and a curtain was drawn, so she couldn't tell the time of day. But a cuckoo clock hung on one wall. She squinted, but it was too far to see the little arms.

The clock reminded her of her bed and breakfast. Her

sisters. She sat up on the couch and swore. They must be so worried. She had to get back to them. She wrapped the fur around her, with every intention of walking across the room to gather her things.

But when she looked down, there was a strange mark on her chest. Gold paint? She licked her finger and tried to rub it off.

"What the fuck?" she said in an exhale.

In a flash, she was plunged into that cold, dark water again. It was the big empty, the nothing that contrasted with everything living and bright. And just before she'd been too tired to fight, there had been a burst of sunshine. A light so bright and warm and good that she had no choice but to follow it back.

Sleep, sunshine.

His words were as clear as the water that had tried to claim her.

And then, there he was again. Her winter god. Her savior. Everything about him was too big, too otherworldly. It was like the cabin had shrunk at his presence. When he entered the living room, she caught a glimpse of a kitchen. She was starving. But she momentarily felt a different kind of hunger when she looked at him again.

He'd gotten dressed, stuffing himself into a pair of trousers that were far too small for his beefy thighs. His cream-colored sweater clung to every single line of his expertly carved body. The leather suspenders attached to the trousers seemed highly unnecessary in light of how fitted his clothes were. What surprised Lia most of all was not the wolf-like curl of his mouth or the golden flecks in his eyes, but the wooden tray clutched in his massive hands. The porcelain teacups in particular looked ridiculous and adorable at the same time.

Fuck, how was she noticing the *teacups* when he was striding toward her, his intense stare locked on her?

She bunched up the furs around her and made a little

whimpering sound. She had so many things she wanted to say, but her tongue wouldn't shape, *"Thank you for saving my life. By the way, who are you?"*

Instead, she pointed at the polar bear and asked, "Is that real?"

He stifled a smile and set down the tray on the coffee table. She realized that there was no teapot in sight, but a label-less bottle of amber liquid.

"You needn't worry, sunshine. It can't hurt you, even if you look good enough to eat," he said.

Lia opened and shut her mouth. She pursed her lips together. She didn't appreciate him teasing her. *Clearly* the thing was dead. At least the irritation that came with his comment shook her out of her stupor.

"There will be no eating," she said, crossing her arms over her chest. "Of *anything*."

"Then I'll settle for drinking." He pulled out the cork with his straight white teeth and poured them each a cup.

"Wait." Lia shook her head. A pinprick of pain struck at her temple. Her stomach betrayed her and made a hungry noise. "Wait. As much as I'd like to start my morning with a shot of what looks like bathtub bourbon, I need some answers."

He set his molten gold eyes on her, trailing her bare shoulders, the way she fidgeted as her skin grew too tight from anxiety and worry. Why did he have to look at her so attentively? Like he was counting the beauty marks across her clavicle or the tiny scar that cut right on her chin from the time she'd fallen from the monkey bars and gotten five stitches.

No one had looked at her like that before. Not any man she'd dated. Not even George.

The winter god picked up a teacup and offered one to her. "Give me your questions, then, darling."

Sunshine. Darling. Who was this man, and why did she feel like leaning toward him every time he murmured those words?

"Who are you?"

"Alexander Nikolas, Sw—" he cut himself off and stopped the teacup at his lips. Surprise fluttered his dark lashes, like he was just realizing something terrible. "Just Alexander. You are?"

"Noelia Luz Espinoza." She didn't know why she felt compelled to offer her middle name. She offered her hand, and he stared at it. She held that inquisitive stare, forcing herself not to look away.

He did not shake her hand, though. His calloused fingertips were gentle as he lowered himself and brushed a kiss across her knuckles. She felt the warm exhale on her skin and a flutter in her tummy.

Then she remembered the rough words he'd uttered when he was trying to save her life. *Crawl to me.* Why did that make her heart flutter?

"It's my turn, Noelia Luz Espinoza." He released her hand and sat back, resting a fist on his thigh. "How, in the name of the bloody saint, did you find yourself in that torrent?"

She gave him a nervous smile. "It's a long story. But right now, I need to reach my sisters. And some clothes, so I'm not wearing a lynx or whatever this was. Not that I'm ungrateful, but you didn't happen to save my bag, too? It's brown, leather. Very sensible satchel?"

Alexander watched her for a moment longer. Did he think her strange? His lip quirked, and she wasn't sure if he was suppressing a laugh or a frown. Either way, he got up, went to retrieve her satchel and a stack of clothes from the closet under the stairs.

"Your other clothes are still wet," he said, handing over her belongings. "But these will do for now."

Lia was overwhelmed with his kindness. He didn't know her from a hole in the wall, but here he was, tending to her.

She tugged on the long sleeve wool sweater. It was the softest thing she'd ever had on her skin. She caught him looking at her hard nipples, and her entire body flashed hot. She set the pants aside and decided to finish dressing when she had more privacy. What she needed was to tell her sisters where she was.

She unzipped her bag, relieved she'd taken out her notebook and supplies. The only things inside were a clump of wet receipts, the ornament she'd bought at the market, and the bag of toiletries she hadn't had a chance to unpack. Frantically, she rummaged in every pocket for her phone, but her memory was frayed with her nerves and near-death experience.

"Your coat was making a terrible sound," Alexander told her, taking a sip of whisky as he watched her with curious amusement.

Relief washed over her as she pulled out her phone. Her sisters had teased her for how decidedly unstylish her waterproof gear was. But here, it had at least kept the worst damage away. But her phone, in its protective waterproof case, was pristine. She still had zero service, but during the night, messages had come through. Helena, Gracie, George, her parents, work. A knot formed at her throat.

She swiped the screen open and typed a message to her sisters: Freak storm. I'm fine. Call when I can.

The message didn't send. "Fuck. There's no wifi here, is there?"

He stared at her like she'd sprouted a second set of arms. "What is why-fy?"

That's when it struck her. The thing she didn't want to poke at because her trauma-brain hadn't processed information correctly. It couldn't have because how was she supposed to rationalize what she'd seen? Alexander had appeared from thin air in a burst of light. A solar flare? A lightning strike? Followed by the most beautiful, pouty man she'd ever seen in her life dressed in a red, embroidered tailcoat, riding astride a...reindeer.

No. There was no way.

She shook her head and decided there had to be a better explanation, and not her wild imagination.

"Alex," she said, her voice tense as she absently touched the golden mark on her skin. "Where did you come from?"

He sat on the armchair beside her and leaned forward on his elbows. "What do you remember?"

"I—I didn't see or hear you. It's like the sky opened, and you came right through. But that's not possible, is it?"

She breathed fast and steady as she waited for his answer. Part of her wanted him to admit that it was a bizarre occurrence of global climate change. But deep down in her heart, a part of her that had wished for a wild adventure when she was a little girl wanted him to say something else. Something truly impossible.

He took a long drink of his whisky then held her gaze with his. "I came from the Eternal Winter Forest, which lies on the other side of the Hallowed Path, the gateway between my home and your world. I am—I was a prince of the realm, son of Saint Nikolas. Now I am exiled."

Lia blinked. And blinked. And then blinked again. Her emotions see-sawed from *what the flying fuck* to *oh, that makes sense*. Because how could it make sense that the most beautiful man she'd ever laid eyes on and had sprung from a *gateway* just in time to save her life was a son of *Saint Nikolas*.

"*Saint* Nikolas," she repeated, grabbing onto the arm of the settee because the room seemed to undulate.

"Everyone in my family bears the name of the saint who

propagated our line." He nodded, like it was the most normal thing in the world.

"Are you trying to tell me that your ancestor was *Santa Claus?*"

He glowered with irritation. "I suppose this realm has its own legends of my world, my ancestor. All of them absolutely absurd."

She reached back into her bag and extracted the trinket she'd bought at the Christmas market before everything had gone to shit. She held the tiny, fat, red-cheeked jolly Ol' Saint Nick in front of Alex's face. "You don't look like this."

Alexander snatched the tiny ornament from her and grimaced. "Neither did the first Saint Nikolas. Though, Nikolas VI *does* bear this resemblance."

"I don't know if you're fucking with me or if you're telling the truth." She rubbed her palms across her face.

"If I fucked with you, you'd know it," he said, his voice dark and playful. "And you'd be less cross than you are right now."

"I'm not *cross*. I'm freaking out," she amended. She tugged down the collar of her sweater. "Did you do this to me?"

Her words were not accusatory. She was in the liminal space between disbelief and wonder.

He poured himself more whisky. "Aye."

"Why?"

"To save your life," he said gruffly, flexing his left hand. "*Again*, I might add."

"Breakfast of champions." She finally picked up her whisky-filled teacup and drank. Her entire body shivered as it warmed down her esophagus and into her empty stomach. She was just making one good decision after the other. "Look, I'm grateful that you saved me. I'm just having a little bit of a hard time believing."

"It's best if you don't," he said, looking away. "That world, that life is behind me. For now, we must focus on surviving this. The storm has ebbed, but snow still falls. We need firewood and food. The guardian hasn't replenished the stores in some time, it seems."

"I think I have an emergency protein bar," she said, reaching back into her bag, then cursed herself. It was on the table at the B&B.

Alexander stood, dusting his trousers. "Stay here. I'll return."

Lia had made a hundred lists, a thousand lists to prepare herself throughout her life. She made back to school lists. "Books to read before I die" lists. Lists rating every kiss she'd ever had—all five of them. She'd made a survival list for the summer Helena dated a guy who loved camping. She prided herself on always being prepared. But in less than twenty-four hours, she'd experienced things she'd never even imagined could have happened to her.

But she was sure of one thing—being left alone in a cabin in the middle of the Black Forest during a blizzard was never, *ever* going to be on any list.

"I'm coming with you." She forgot about her self-imposed shame and tugged on her underwear and borrowed wool trousers.

"The hell you are," he grunted, tossing her ornament on the table. The tiny wooden Santa Claus fell into his empty cup.

"Well, you can't leave me alone."

He stopped on his way to the front door. "Can you hunt?"

She licked her teeth, irritation narrowing her eyes. "No."

"Can you chop wood?"

"I can pick up loose branches."

"Then you're no use to me."

"And I say I'm coming with you." Lia crossed her arms. She

felt the heat of his stare as her tits pushed up with the movement, her nipples still hard enough to cut glass.

She didn't know why she felt so bold suddenly. Was it him? Was it easier to be someone different in front of a stranger? Or was it that she'd almost died, and she had zero fucks left to give?

Whatever the reason, she couldn't take no for an answer. He was just as frustrated with her as she was with him. He'd gone out of his way to keep her safe. But the idea of staying behind, of waiting for him to return made her queasy. The snap of bold anger vanished as quickly as it came.

"Please," she said softly. "I won't get in your way. I just—I don't want to be alone."

He let go of a frustrated grunt, raking his fingers through his short, dark hair. "Very well. You can collect firewood for kindling. But stay close to me. I don't fancy another swim."

She resented that comment and pulled on a borrowed fur coat and hat, shooting daggers his way as he propped opened a trunk and brought out a quiver of arrows and a carved bow. He opened the door, and a gust of wind slammed against them.

"Last chance, darling," he murmured in her ear.

Lia stared at the forest beyond the door, the blanket of white. Fear twisted in her belly, and something else. Something she'd never quite felt before. *Excitement.* A thrilling sensation that burned her up like the whisky sloshing in her stomach.

And so, Lia Espinoza took her first step out of the cabin and back into the unknown.

6

ALEXANDER

"It's not too late to turn back," Alexander told her. *Noelia.* The pretty vowels of her name were at the tip of his tongue. He wanted to say her name out loud, to hear her answer to him. To have her impossibly dark eyes on him and only him.

But she was already frightened, and he did not want to add to that. Part of him knew he shouldn't have let her come along. The blizzard had passed, but the snow hadn't stopped falling, and if he didn't mark the trees, they could get lost.

They hadn't walked far, keeping to the right side of the narrow stone wall that marked the border between the Eternal Winter Forest and the human world. Her breathing was already labored. She hadn't rested enough after her ordeal. When he glanced back, he forced himself to scowl and rubbed his lips together to stop from laughing. Elowen's coat was large on her, the hat falling over her eyes.

"I'm fine," she huffed.

"You look like a drunk bear."

She grumbled and raised her middle finger at him. "And

you look like a lost member from *Magic Mike: The Holiday Special*."

"Is he a great sorcerer?"

Noelia caught up to him in three heavy steps and let loose a howling laugh. He wanted to remind her that he'd never be able to catch so much as a mushroom if she wasn't quiet. Only, he couldn't make himself do it because he rather liked the sound of that terrible laugh.

"Right," she said, raising her eyebrows. "You probably don't have movies in your Santa kingdom."

Alexander stopped and pinched the air. "It's the Eternal Winter Forest."

"I'll have to see it to believe it."

He thought about the things he'd seen when he'd warmed her body with his magic. She struck him as someone who was filled with dreams. Joy. Perhaps that had been her in the past. He hadn't regretted healing her, but now he was concerned about making the Mark of the Saint spread.

"Does your hand hurt?" she asked.

"Hmm?"

"Your hand. You keep massaging your palm. Did you hurt yourself?"

Was that concern in her deep, dark eyes? Why should she care about him being hurt? He was larger than she was, stronger. He could take a beating and worse. And yet she'd noticed the way he absently touched the root of the Mark.

"It doesn't hurt," he admitted.

"That wasn't there before," she said, trudging through the powdery snow that came up to her knees. "When you held out your hand the first time, that mark wasn't there."

He said nothing, only listened to the sounds of the woods. The whistles of branches slapping against the wind. Their breath, and stride, became syncopated. Part of him wanted to tell her about the Mark. But that would mean telling her about why he'd run, that he had been a coward, that he'd seen his brother die and left. She already looked at him like he was miraculous. He didn't want that to change. Did he?

It didn't matter. As long as the Mark didn't get completed by the winter solstice, which was that very night, he'd be safe. He'd be free.

"You never told me how you came to be alone in a blizzard," he said.

She gnawed on her lower lip. He found himself wondering how that mouth would feel between his teeth, how he could suck that pretty, full pout and banish all her worries with a lick of his tongue. He had the urge to shove her against the hard trunk of a tree and make all their troubles go away for a moment, fleeting. Too fleeting.

"It's a long story," she said, repeating what she had hours prior.

"I want to hear your long story, Noelia."

"It's Lia." She smiled. After a moment of hesitation, she relented. "Prepare yourself for the most dramatic, ridiculous tale that will make you regret having saved my life."

He heard the humor in her voice, but he frowned at the thought that he'd ever regret what had transpired between them.

She launched into an explanation of a marriage proposal, a journey that brought her to this human region she called the Black Forest, and the consequently failed engagement. She'd run away, just as he had. Both of them were attempting to outrun their fates.

"You are not ridiculous," he said, as much in defense of her as himself and his own action.

When she looked up at him with those big, innocent brown eyes, he nearly staggered in the snow. It would have been worth it to have her look at him that way, like they were in on a secret together. Them against the rest of the world who would change them into people they didn't know how to be.

"Thanks for saying that," she said. "I thought that I would have planned every detail of my life. My parents didn't make plans. Everything they did was out of necessity. But I've had a bucket list since I could write."

"What exactly is on this bucket list? I presume buckets?"

She snorted. "No, it's a list of things I want to do."

"Like a quest of sorts?" he asked, genuinely curious.

"Sort of. Soul searching in Machu Picchu would be sort of a quest."

"I went on a quest when I was seventeen to prove to my father that I was worthy."

"Worthy of what?"

He let the silence stretch. Surveyed the still woods ahead of them. "Simply worthy. He tasked me with retrieving the heart of the Elfenhörn Forest. It's a mythical plant that grants eternal life. I failed. I wasn't worthy."

"That's cruel."

Hearing her say those words, words that would have been treason in his kingdom, felt like taking a deep breath after nearly drowning.

"My father was very hard on us," he said. "On me."

"Same." She tugged on that lip again, and it drove him mad how much he wanted to be the one to worry that pout. "The worst part is I wonder if my father gave George his blessing, not because he'll make me happy but because it might be the solution to the family restaurant. To make sure I don't struggle like my parents did. But that's not enough."

Alexander's mood grew dark. He didn't know this George, but he loathed the idea of Noelia marrying him. Not because he cared, but because he didn't believe that anyone should be forced into such a union.

"I'm no expert on love," he admitted. "Is he terrible, this George fellow?"

"He's not, like, a puppy killer or anything." Lia kept up with his pace more easily then. The blue stone wall of the Hallowed Path peeked under the snow to their left. "The truth is, I don't know much about him, deep down where it counts. I don't know what his favorite song is or what he's afraid of. I know he likes his steak well done and he drinks one glass of pinot noir at dinner. I know that he never curses, and he cares about what his coworkers think of him. I know that when I asked him if he loved me, he didn't say yes."

"He sounds like a monster," Alexander said, exaggerating the word. Then after she didn't laugh, he added, "He sounds like he doesn't know you."

"Neither do you."

He stopped walking and turned to her. "Perhaps. But I do know that you would not be happy with half a life, an expected life. I know you traveled far from your home simply because you chose yourself and choosing yourself is a brave thing to do. Even when it might hurt."

"Oh," she sighed, her eyes flicking up to his lips. "It sounds nicer when you say it."

If he lowered his face just a bit, he could kiss her. But that wasn't what she needed. She was confused and bearing her soul, and his mind kept conjuring images of her bare shoulders wrapped in furs. The wind tossed her hair over her face, and he allowed himself the pleasure of brushing it behind her ear, then balled his hand into a fist to stay his touch.

The snap of a twig drew their attention. He pressed his finger to his lips and motioned for her to crouch low at the base of a tree.

At the bottom of the slope was a doe eating frost-covered berries from the other side of the Hallowed Path. Alexander drew an arrow and aimed. If he made the shot, it would be a quick death. He exhaled low and watched the way the condensation blew. And then he let the arrow fly.

Antlers appeared out of nowhere and knocked the arrow away. The doe leapt across the wall, and Alexander strung together a series of curses as Kilian stomped his forelegs.

"Do you realize what you've done?" Alexander shouted at the reindeer. All at once he realized his friend was not supposed to be there. "Why are you here? You are free from your vow! Go home, Kilian!"

The reindeer snuffed and bared its teeth at Alexander.

"She's a doe, not of the Elfenhörn!"

"Are you talking to your reindeer?" Lia asked beside him.

Alexander loosed a low, impatient growl. "My very self-righteous friend here just cost us our dinner."

Kilian whimpered, and an apology was already on Alexander's tongue when the reindeer hopped over the blue wall and vanished into the trees.

"Alexander?" Lia said softly.

"Not now," the self-exiled prince of the Eternal Winter Forest said. He was making a mess of things. But he felt the strangeness in Lia's voice when she uttered his name.

When he turned around, he saw it. Several animals had emerged from their burrows and tree hollows. Owls perched on branches, and squirrels scampered up trunks. A rafter of fat turkeys waddled nearby.

"What in the Beast Master hell is happening?" Lia whispered.

He knew what was drawing these creatures out. He'd gone hunting with his father when all they'd had to do was stand there and stroll through the Queen's Forest until the critters appeared to them. That wretched mark, the power of Nikolas, the magic that drew animals to it. He hadn't considered it would work outside of the kingdom.

Alexander drew another arrow, looked up at the blanket of snow clouds. Flakes kissed his face, and he whispered the prayer of the hunt—"Oh, ye, Father, thank thee for this bounty, of your blood and bones. Glorious is the Eternal Winter."

This time, he did not miss.

He felled two turkeys. He waded through the snow to retrieve his prize and whispered a final thanks to the creatures as the others dispersed.

"Alexander," came Lia's voice, again, this time tight with fear.

He saw the shadow first. When he whirled around, he was startled by the sight of a creature he'd only ever read about. A shadow sylph. Creatures of air and shadow. This one took the shape of a wolf, baring black fangs and long claws.

Forest animals hadn't been the only things that had been drawn to Alexander's sainted mark. The monsters had, too.

7
LIA

"We're safe," Alexander said, stepping slowly toward her, placing his body like a shield. "It can't cross the Hallowed Path."

The shadow monster stalked out of the trees on the other side of the blue wall. It took the shape of a feral wolf, but when it hit an invisible wall, it dispersed into a mass of shapeless darkness.

"Start heading back to the cabin," Alexander said. "I'll keep it distracted."

His even breath came out in clouds, and she convinced herself that they were safe. That barrier was keeping the thing caged in.

She didn't want to leave him, but she was not going to argue when it came to a literal shadow monster threatening them both. Lia trembled as she retraced the footprints they'd left in the snow. She counted them, one at a time, the way she counted when she was having an anxiety attack.

Telling herself not to look back, she knew it was useless. She had to look. Make sure Alexander was all right. He'd dropped the turkeys and drawn another arrow. The creature was solidifying in shape again, this time into a massive scorpion, its sharp pincers stabbing at the wall. It broke apart, then reformed back into a wolf.

"Lia," Alexander's voice warbled. "Run. Please, *run*."

He'd be fine, wouldn't he? He was over six feet tall and practically carved out of marble. He'd be fine. He had to be. She was soft and decidedly unmagical, *if* his stories could be believed. Witnessing the demonic wolf, how could she not believe?

Lia took off, though running wasn't what she'd call whatever she was doing. The snow was too high, the wind picking up again.

"Stupid pristine nature and its stupid inconvenient wind!"

Lia got a few feet, panting her little heart out. She peered back just in time to see the creature break through the invisible wall. Sharp canines snarled from black gums. Glowing moon eyes locked on Alexander.

The wolf was on him before she could scream. He pried its jaws apart with his bare hands, the creature struggling to get free.

"Fuck me," she said, already running back to help, picking up a thick discarded branch.

Heart hammering, mouth dry, she gathered every bit of the anxiety and fear coursing through her veins. She turned all of that into her own fuel, closed the distance between her and the wolf, and swung with both arms.

The branch split in half against its back. The creature's attention snapped to her, giving Alexander the opportunity to take better hold of its maw.

"I told you to run!"

"You're not the prince of me."

Lia threw herself to the ground and picked up an arrow that had fallen from his quiver. She was hopeless to think fear would turn her into Katniss, magic or not. She didn't need to aim and shoot. Lia just needed a little bit of strength as she screamed and jammed the arrow into the wolf's eye.

The monster whined and rolled off Alexander. Blood dripped from his hands and pebbled the snow into rubies.

The wolf righted itself in seconds and lunged again. Alexander caught it around the middle, and they fell. Fists and claws drawing blood and bruises. Lia searched the empty forest for help. She dug her cold hands into the pockets of her borrowed coat and found something metal. A knife!

She shouted Alexander's name and threw it. Alexander caught it mid-air. As he raised his fist for a final blow, the wolf wrung itself free and made a bull's eye toward Lia.

Lia could hear her pulse in her ear drums. She turned and ran. She knew she'd never be fast enough. Heat and pain spiked up her legs, and she fell, crawling through the snow. Pain tore through her calves. Her throat hurt from her own desperate screams.

And then, there was a wet, slick sound, followed by the crunch of bones.

Shaking, Lia blinked the snow out of her eyes.

Alexander rose above her. His sweater was ripped to ribbons, and his torso was covered in the beast's blood. He winced, and she followed his eyes to the tattoo burning its way over the mound of his hand and an inch up the inside of his wrist.

"You saved me," she said. "Again."

"This time, you saved me first." Alexander offered her a pained smile. "We have to stop making this a habit."

He gathered the arrows and bow and slung them over his shoulder. She picked up the dead turkeys, and Alexander hefted her into his arms. She considered toughing it out and walking, but she didn't want to draw attention to the pain in her calf, not when he looked like he'd played Seven Minutes in Heaven with Edward Scissor Hands.

"What was that thing?" Lia asked, casting a final glance at the place where the wolf broke apart into mulch and ooze, melting the snow beneath it.

Alexander was quiet for a long time. They fell into the rhythm of her sighs, his heavy steps, a random owl hooting along their walk back to the cabin.

"It's a shadow sylph. Ancient spirits that lived in the Eternal Winter Kingdom thousands of years ago. I've only ever heard stories of them. It never should have broken through the wall."

The way that the monster had gone right for Alexander made her realize there was more to his exile than he was telling her. She didn't want to press, not after the couple of days they'd had.

When they arrived at the cabin moments later, the warmth was gone, and the fireplace was dead.

"We got everything except firewood," she said, holding onto each turkey by the neck. She thought of Alexander going back out there, and bile rose to her throat.

As if he were reading her mind, Alexander turned to the mouth of the fireplace. He closed his eyes and extended his hands like he was warming his palms. Only, there was no fire to warm.

Lia felt the pressure in the air change. A breeze that shouldn't have been there circled around him. He rubbed his palms together, and a burst of light kindled in the space between his palms. He threw that flame into the heart of the fireplace where it was suspended in the air.

"That should last us for the night," he said, clenching his jaw so the muscle there rippled.

Again, the tattoo etched vines and leaves several inches up

and around his wrist. She wanted to ask him what that was, why he looked so angry because of it, but he spoke first.

"You're hurt." He pointed to her lower leg. Blood was seeping through the gray fabric.

"It's just a scratch," she said and tried to walk past him, then felt the floor undulate beneath her.

"Lia," he said, then shouted her name. She was aware of him holding her upright. His hand was around her waist and her palms resting on the swell of his pectorals. Then the world snapped back into place. "Lia?"

"I'm fine. We have to get that turkey in the oven or we're going to starve, and you'll just have to listen to my stomach making hungry noises all night long." She ran a finger over the smooth skin exposed by his torn shirt. "Oh, you're *so* soft."

His lips twitched, but he didn't let himself smile. "You are a stubborn thing."

He took the turkeys into the kitchen then returned for her. She weighed nothing in his arms as he carried her up the stairs and into the bathroom. Copper pipes lined one wall, and a giant tub was nestled in one corner. He opened the faucet and let steaming water fill the tub.

He sat Lia up on the sink and tore the seam of her trousers. She gasped at the swift movement and the way her body tightened at his strength.

"I've never quite met someone who was so surprised by everything," he said.

"Well, it's not every day I learn that magic is real and that the heir of Santa Claus saved my life several times."

He frowned, but not at what she'd said. Up on her thigh were four thin claw marks.

"Gracie has a cat that scratched me worse than this." Even as she spoke the words, she knew something was different. Her heartbeat was too fast, her body scorching, like she was burning from the inside out. It was a good kind of heat, though. Like it was made of thick, hot chocolate.

He rested a hand on her knee and pushed it to the side. She felt a flutter between her legs. Alexander licked his bottom lip. It was a good lip, plump like a ripe berry and just as pink.

"What are you doing?" she whispered.

"Your pupils are dilated, and you're warm to the touch," he said, pressing the back of his hand to her forehead. "I'm searching for—ah—there it is."

He pushed back the ripped fabric of her trousers and lifted her leg, exposing her calf. A small piece of a broken fang was wedged into the muscle. Deep purple and black veins had begun to spread like spiderwebs.

"You can't feel that?" he asked.

She nodded slightly. "I didn't want you to think I was weak."

Alexander's golden eyes softened. He brushed her hair back. His touch felt so good against her temples. "I would never judge your pain, darling."

"You hide your pain," she said, brushing her finger on the inside of his wrist.

A frown creased his forehead. "That's different. You're human. I'm—"

"A winter god?"

He unbuckled his suspender and handed it to her. "Bite down on this."

"How about I bite down on your—" She clapped her hands over her mouth. "Why am I saying that?"

"The poison is a strange one. Sylphs are spirits of air. Some have mischievous impulses, tricky and playful. Others are more malevolent. They're pure energy, pure desire, or so the stories say. The more its poison spreads, the more you want to give in to your baser impulses."

"Is that bad?" She felt that flutter again, an ache building between her thighs.

He reached behind her and retrieved a crude pair of tweezers from the top shelf. "Not at first. At first it might even feel good to let go, to do whatever your body craves. But then, after your body has had enough—enough pleasure, enough pain—your heart gives out."

"Oh," she whimpered.

She bit down on the leather strap and seized his shoulder as he bent down between her legs and plucked the evil tooth from her calf. She moaned at the pain that bloomed between her eyes and the way he cradled her leg.

"There, you're all right," he whispered at her ear.

She grabbed hold of his shoulder, pulling him closer to her so he was nestled between her thighs.

"Hold on, foolish darling."

She made a whining sound. "There's more?"

"I can't very well leave you with an open wound, can I?"

Lia was aware that it was the effect of the poison in her system, but his voice felt like the crush of velvet on her skin. He squeezed her hip to keep her in place as he palmed her wound. She gasped at the heat of his touch, at the magic that he pushed into her flesh. This time, she saw the threads that connected them, the ancient gift stitching her wound back together and purging the venom away.

She saw flashes of Alex as a boy running in a dark forest. Alex training in an empty armory. Alex getting hit by a man with his same golden eyes, only they held none of the same warmth.

She was overcome with the need to soothe him, so she scooted up against him. They were lined up so perfectly, she felt the rigid length straining against his trousers. She sought the friction of him against her. She had never done this, never felt a man hard for her.

"Fuck," he whispered, grinding back into her, then pushing himself off. He shook his head. "I'm sorry. I shouldn't— You're hurt."

She brushed the golden print of his hand that marked her calf. "You healed me. I'm fine."

Alexander took a step back toward her but stopped when they heard the splash. The tub was overflowing. He tore himself from her, turned off the faucet, and emptied a bottle of oil and soap into the water.

"Get in," he told her, a slight tremble to his voice. "It'll help with—"

"Please don't leave me," she said softly. She gnawed nervously on her lip. She wasn't sure what she wanted from him, but she knew that she didn't want him to go. It was ridiculous how she had the courage to face a shadow sylph but couldn't find the words to say exactly what she wanted.

She wanted to feel him again. She wanted him to touch her. She wanted the heat of his magic and to know more about the memories that flooded between them.

Instead, she cleared her throat and said, "You're dirty, too. I mean, I just don't want to be alone. We don't have to do anything. I've never been— I've never done—"

"Lia," he said, achingly patient. He grabbed her chin and traced the tiny scar there. "I'm not going anywhere."

He turned around and undressed. He'd already lost his sweater and torn most of his trousers. She quickly shed her clothes and waded into the hot, soapy water. Eucalyptus and pine steam cleared her sinuses. She gathered her hair atop her head and glanced at the sweep of his lower back and muscular ass.

When he heard the splash of water, he waited a heartbeat, then turned to her. She tried to look anywhere. The strange orbs of light on the ceiling. The creaky copper pipes. But she failed. Alexander had a rugged kind of beauty. Muscles that were hard-earned but not overly defined. Masculine and strong, with a dark trail of hair leading to his cock. Even semi-hard, he was thick and long, with a dusky pink tip. She felt an ache deep in her pussy as he stepped into the tub and his legs brushed against hers.

Facing each other, with arms dangling over the sides of the tub, Lia settled into that moment. She was naked with a man. She'd never been naked with anyone. George had been the first guy to see her in her bra, but that and some kissing was as far as they'd gotten. To stop her George-related spiral, she grabbed a bar of soap and lathered it up in her hands, dragging it across her chest and up and down her arms.

She saw a feral spark in his eyes, the kind she'd seen in the eyes of the shadow wolf. Hunger. She liked it when he looked at her that way. More than liked it. She was beginning to wonder how she would ever do without it.

Emboldened by his stare and the way he gripped the sides of the tub, Lia sat up on her knees. Her small breasts peeked out of the surface, but he kept his molten gaze fixed on hers.

"May I?" she asked, holding the soap over his chest.

He swallowed hard and nodded.

Lia wetted the bar of soap and washed away the dirt and blood, leaving behind bruised skin mottled with green, blue, and purple. He shut his eyes as she trailed his arms, his shoulders.

"No one has ever touched me like this," he whispered. She noticed the strained muscles of his throat, as if it cost him something to admit those words.

"Well," she said, "this is a first for me, too."

"Come here," he said, the sound of desperation in his command.

She sat back between his legs. He let go of a deep grunt. His erect cock was wedged between them, resting at the small of her back. She was careful not to move, not to do more than let him lather her skin clean, even though she felt filthy with the pressure of him against her. She leaned back, exposing her breasts to the cool air. She grabbed Alexander's hand and guided it back to the golden handprint on her skin. He smoothed the spot there, and she wondered if he could feel how hard her heart was beating. He lathered her breasts, brushing his thumb over the stiff buds of her dark brown nipples.

She'd been so good about keeping her moans to herself, but he felt too good, and she couldn't help it. He did it again, and again, bringing his lips to the inner curve of her throat as he pinned her to him.

He made her feel like her skin was on fire, and he hadn't even touched her everywhere. He was simply making her feel good, without rushing or pushing. She didn't know touch could feel that way, feel so much.

Lia leaned her head back against his chest. She ran a finger along the inside of his left wrist. "Tell me about your mark."

Whatever spell they had conjured, broke. As he unstopped the drain and let the murky bathwater run out, she worried she'd said the wrong thing. That he was leaving her there, frustrated and curious and naked. Then he turned on the shower, and lukewarm water rained overhead. Alexander's silence spoke volumes. He was thoughtful, and she knew that when he finally spoke it was because he was ready to share a part of himself with her.

"Long ago, Saint Nikolas of Myra became disappointed with the world," he started. "No matter how hard he tried, people gave in to their darkest wants, deepest sins. So he went into exile, and his loyal followers went with him. They searched for solitary islands up in the deepest north. Traveled through sea and mountain and woods until they reached the Elfennhörn Forest."

"The forest on the other side of that blue wall?"

He lathered the bar of soap on his head and then handed it to her. "Exactly. There were forest fae there. Folk of the trees and sky."

"Fairies?"

"They called themselves Elfenhörn. Spirits of nature. Saint Nikolas and his people were welcomed. When they discovered his God-given gifts—of resurrection—of alchemy—they offered him a boon. If he destroyed the evil in the forest, he would be crowned king."

"I'm guessing he did," she said.

"The Eternal Winter Kingdom flourished, a paradise among the realms. There is no disease, no sin, no evil. We don't even have dungeons."

Lia frowned. It sounded too good to be true, but she let him finish. He told her of how Saint Nikolas imbued his two sons with great power, leaving all others, like Alex, as the spares.

"Then why did you leave," she asked.

Water rained over, washing away all traces of suds. That's when she saw the raw hurt on his features. He'd told her he was exiled. The realization hit her even before he explained.

"My brother was murdered, and I ran like the fires of hell were at my heels. My brother died because I failed at my duty. Because I wasn't there." He shut the faucet, and they stood there for a moment, more naked and exposed than ever. "I ran because I did not want the Mark of the Saint to take root, but every time I summon the power of the Nikolas, the more it spreads."

Lia traced the golden imprint of his magic on her chest. "I'm sorry. You used your power to heal me. I'm so sorry, Alexander."

"I'm not. I would do it again and again if it meant keeping you in this world because now that I know you, I cannot imagine a world without you in it." He cupped her face and whispered a kiss on her lips. He pulled away before she could chase him into the kind of deep kiss that would ruin her. "Now I simply have to outlast the winter solstice tonight, and then I will be free of this curse. After—I do not know. Perhaps I'll make one of your lists of buckets."

Lia grinned and laughed deeply. She could think of one new item she'd added to her own list. And he was standing right in front of her.

"Oh," she said. "Now you're speaking my language."

8

ALEXANDER

Alexander needed to get a grip on himself. Literally. His balls ached with the need to release. Lia had gone from demurely covering her naked chest with furs that morning to guiding his fucking hand over her pert little nipples. The moment he left the bathing room, he hurried downstairs. Yes, he needed more clothes, but his body thrummed with the urgent need to fuck.

He took his pulsing cock in hand and barely made it to the fireplace, where the waves of heat flogged his bare skin and he spent his semen into the flames. He looked up into the frozen face of Elowen's prized polar bear head and felt the same kind of shame he had when he could barely walk around the palace out of fear that a stray gust of wind would have his maypole straining.

He found new clothes and shoved himself into the wool leggings and sweater. He looked utterly ridiculous, and there was little he could do to hide his bulge no matter what borrowed pants he donned. Not that Lia seemed to mind.

Even the memory of her grinding her pussy against him was enough to make him hard again. He needed to expel his pent-up

THE HEART OF WINTER

energy, and so while Lia dressed, he went out back, trudged through the snow, and chopped down the nearest tree he could find. The wind howled, but the surrounding forest was otherwise still. Too still. It left room for his chaotic thoughts that kept returning to the unbelievable woman waiting in the cabin.

As he split the tree trunk into stackable logs, Alexander reminded himself that he had been with hundreds of people. He took pride in giving pleasure. What made him hesitate with Lia? Was he being delicate with her because he'd held her fragile life in his hands several times?

She hadn't been fragile when she'd fought the shadow sylph. Even that memory, violent and bloody, her lovely face set with fierce determination, made him hard. He craned his head to the afternoon sun, safely hidden behind snow clouds, and begged for mercy.

Mercy for the inexplicable, strange feelings waging a war within him. Alexander had a new life to start. He'd said goodbye to Hans, to his kingdom, to Kilian. He rubbed at a bruise that ached over his chest when he thought of saying goodbye to Lia.

Perhaps, the thought sprouted in the recesses of his mind. *Perhaps he wouldn't have to.*

9
LIA

Lia had never been as painfully aware of her virginity as she was in that moment after Alexander left her naked in the shower. Part of her had wanted him to ravish her, to explore her as he had in that tub. Then he'd revealed the story of why he'd run away instead, and it was a different kind of intimacy. One she wasn't used to with someone who wasn't family.

She didn't like being away from her sisters, especially without being able to let them know she was safe, but for the first time since she fell through the ice, she wondered if the little cabin tucked away under the snowstorm was exactly where they needed to be. An in-between place. A bridge between the things they were running from and toward.

Lia twisted the brown glass bottles of oils and rubbed it all over her skin and the ends of her hair. She smelled like a meadow, the scents more floral than the soft vanilla and coconut she was used to spritzing every morning. When she massaged the oil over her breasts, she felt restless at the memory of Alexander's touch.

She cringed at how she'd acted under the heady rush of that

poison. Even now, she was warm and languid. She needed to get a grip.

Lia dressed and hurried to the kitchen to find something to eat. There was a tin of stale cookies which she devoured in a few bites. She heard the steady rhythm of someone chopping wood, and crept to the window facing the crescent of yard. She cupped her hands to the frosted glass.

Every time Alexander raised the axe overhead, his sweater rode up. His abdominal muscles tightened. For the first time in her life, she wondered what it would be like to be a log. To be split open by him.

"What the hell's the *matter* with you?" she muttered. If he'd wanted her, he would have done something about it. Wouldn't he? "He's a winter god. You're a glorified publicist."

"Who's a winter god?" came the deep, gravelly voice behind her.

Lia whirled around. "Nothing! I mean, I—we—need your wood." She blinked at her own innocent Freudian fumble. "Your *fire*wood. We can't eat raw turkey."

Alexander raised an eyebrow. His breath condensing in shallow pants at the doorway. "Raw turkey is a delicacy in my kingdom."

Lia couldn't keep the twist of horror from her face. "It is?"

They stared at each other for a long beat before he broke down and laughed. Lines crinkled at the corners of his eyes, and he looked younger, unburdened. He shut the door and walked across the kitchen to the oven.

"My apologies, darling." He grabbed a mitt and heaved the oven door open. Flames roared at the back of the grates. "The hearth heats the whole cabin, including this and the water. We should have more than enough firewood."

"Good. Maybe I'll be able to get a signal in the morning."

She was surprised that instead of relief, the idea if leaving made her anxious.

"Aye." He nodded, frowning slightly as he grabbed a giant pot of water and set it to boil. "Have you ever plucked game fowl?"

She scoffed. "I grew up in my a restaurant, and I spent every summer at my grandmother's farm. You better believe my sisters and I learned, or we didn't eat. What about you? Don't princes have servants who cook for them?"

Alexander opened the door to a narrow pantry. It appeared mostly empty, but he returned with a crate of dirt-covered beets, potatoes, and garlic. He didn't meet her eyes as he picked out the skinny purple garlic buds. "The kitchens were my hiding place in the palace. It was warm, and Orenya always let me steal sugar bread, but she ran a tight ship, and if I was going to spend hours there, I had to get earn my place."

"Who were you hiding from?"

"My brothers," he said, matter-of-factly. "Before I got bigger and could hit harder."

He grabbed a turkey by the neck and submerged it in the steaming water. She did the same. When they were finished plucking the feathers and removing the giblets, they decided to cook one and keep the second in the icebox. They worked on opposite ends of the counter, fueled by their hunger, though she stole glances. She caught him, too.

"I've been wondering," she said, "if the kingdom of the North Pole—"

"Eternal Winter Kingdom," he corrected.

"If the Eternal Winter Kingdom is this paradise where there is no sin or evil, then why would your brothers ever hurt you?" *Why would someone commit murder*, she wanted to add.

Alexander clenched his jaw and focused on cleaning the dirt

off the beets and potatoes. "I cannot say, Lia. And that is the most honest answer I can give. I have always suspected that there was something—*wrong*—in our family. Something that made *us* exempt from the values we purported. That there was something rotten in our line, but I never found the root of the rot."

She held a bundle of dried rosemary against her chest. "You're not rotten."

He picked up a cleaver and severed the turkey's neck. "I'm certainly not good."

How could he possibly think that? How could he think that he wasn't *good*? "You saved a total stranger. You could have left me to die."

"I thought of it," he confessed. "There was a moment when you were under the water that I told myself to keep running. No one would find you. No one would know."

Lia hadn't realized that she was moving toward him until she was at his side, resting her hand over his. "You thought of it, and you still chose to help me. That's the difference."

"You defend me, Lia. But you do not know everything I've done."

She shrugged. "It's crazy, I know. And somehow, I think that what I need to know is this. You and me and here."

He stared at her for a long moment, but she only picked up a knife and chopped garlic, humming one of her mom's favorite songs that she played whenever they made family dinner. For the briefest flash, she tried to imagine being in the same position with George—cooking in comfortable silence—and her mind wouldn't conjure the scene. He had never liked making meals at home.

When they were finished dressing the turkey and stuffing it full of herbs, Alexander hefted the tray into the oven.

"There," she said, opening the tin of stale cookies. "Now we just wait for five hours. I can share my cookies in the meantime."

Alexander leaned in close and crinkled his nose. "Knowing Elowen, these have been here for a year. She survives on dried venison, cookies, whisky, and cider."

"A balanced diet." Lia made an exaggerated crunching sound and tapped the crumbs off her lips. "Don't care. Delicious stale Christmas cookies."

"You'll be the death of me," he murmured, chuckling as he retrieved the bottle of what looked like fizzy cider. He poured them each a mug and plopped down at the small kitchen table. "Now, you said you'd help me with my list of buckets, and I expect you to keep this promise."

She rummaged for a pen and paper until she found a small leather-bound notebook and a pencil that looked like it had been whittled by hand.

She wet her finger on her tongue and flipped the pages full of funny cartoons of woodland creatures until she got to a clean page. She wrote "List of buckets" at the very top.

"All right, what have you always wanted to do that you've never done before?"

Alexander seemed startled by that question. He sipped his cider and leaned back, spreading his powerful thighs in a way that drew her attention. Clothes truly were an inconvenience to her horny virgin brain. "I rather believe I've done everything."

"How is that possible?"

Alexander counted on his fingers. "If I want sex, I have it. If I want a quest, I venture out. If I want something, I go and get it."

Lia drank her cider because even the mention of him having sex knit a strange feeling in her belly. The cider was tart and tasted more like the kombucha Gracie liked to drink, but it got better with every sip. "Come on. Perhaps you've done everything in the Christmas Land, but not here. You're in the human realm now."

"Are there many wonders here for me to seek?" he asked.

"Many wonders. My home, New York City. Greatest city in the world. There's the *actual* seven wonders of the world. Though you'll need a passport...and a job...Okay, let's think of this from a new angle. A bucket list is things you want to do before you kick the bucket, you know, *die*."

Alexander blinked his surprise. "The bucket is a symbol of death. Oh, that changes everything."

"Great." She positioned her notebook to dictate his list.

"In that case, I've done it all."

Lia deflated.

"I've climbed the Giant's Bane mountains. I've seen the clash of angels at the furthest point of the kingdom. I've wrestled polar bears. And now I can add that I've been snowed in with a beautiful human who likes stale Christmas cookies."

Lia blinked and processed the fact that he'd called her beautiful. It might seem like a small thing. Helena got called beautiful all the time. But it was different when someone you liked said it out loud. It had her regressing to being young and full of hope that someone might see the real her, the honest to goodness Lia.

"What's the clash of angels?" she asked. "Are there actual angels where you come from?"

He smiled brightly. "It's what we call the light phenomenon that occurs during the summer. The night sky turns into a riot of colors."

"We call it the Northern Lights," she said. "Yours sounds prettier, though."

"What's on your list, then, Lia Espinoza?"

She gently rolled her eyes. "No. Mine seems boring since I don't have *wrestle a polar bear* on mine."

He wagged a finger at her. "You've attacked a mythical shadow sylph and lived to tell the tale."

"Fine," she muttered. She wrote down the list she knew by heart.

Trek Machu Picchu
Swim with turtles
Sail through the Mediterranean Sea
Sleep under the Northern Lights
Get a tattoo
Fall madly in love
Have sex

Lia snorted, remembering that it was Helena who had added "have sex" to the list nearly a year to the date before her 30th birthday. She hadn't noticed Alexander walk around the table to peer over her shoulder. The soft exhale of his breath against her ear made her jump.

"Madly in love?"

"This is not an invitation for critique," she said, defensively. "Helena, my older sister, loves all the time. She falls in love with every pretty face she sees. My youngest sister is the opposite. She doesn't believe in love at all, only chemical brain reactions and hormones."

"And you?" His voice was tense and husky.

"Me." She ran her finger absently over her heart, where the golden imprint of his hand was hidden by her sweater. "I don't know anymore. When I was younger, I was obsessed with love stories. I thought that I'd be at a bookstore and see a guy and we'd reach for the same book, and it would be instant. Or I'd get on the subway car going to Coney Island and meet the man of my dreams on the F train and we'd spend our first day at Luna Park overlooking the ocean." She took a long drink of her cider, but she couldn't quite fill the ache in her heart that was always there. "Then it just never happened. I'd hoped George might be it, but he wasn't. These days, I have to fight for a vintage copy of *Love in the Time of Cholera* at the Strand, and the most action I got on the F train was when a drunk man flashed me his penis."

"What about you?" she asked quickly, to get his attention away from her.

He leaned against a load-bearing wooden beam. The way he crossed his arms while holding his mug accentuated his strength. He tugged on his bottom lip with his teeth, and she imagined what it would feel like to kiss him, truly kiss him.

"I have never had need of love," he said simply.

"Oh." She traced the condensation on her glass.

"And you couldn't love this *George* fellow?" Alexander said George's name with distaste.

"I wanted to. I tried. I hate hurting anyone. And I hate having to make big decisions without thinking them through. I just—thought my life would be different by now."

"And the sex?" Alexander asked.

Lia was halfway through a gulp of her cider when she choked. She cleared her throat and set the glass down, casting an un-amused glare at his crooked smile. "What about it?"

"It's on your list." His face was alight with mischief, otherworldly in the curve of his cheekbones and the fullness of his mouth. "These things are important to you. Important for you to visit, to experience before you die. I'm merely curious as to why sex is important to you."

Lia *could* have died right then and there. She'd nearly experienced literal death three times in almost twenty-four hours. The lake, the shadow wolf, the poison. And none of that was as painful as talking to this man, this descendant of saints, about why she was a virgin. Still, she wrote it down for a reason. Somewhere in her subconscious, she'd wanted him to know.

To give herself time, she basted the turkey then swapped out their ciders for teacup whisky. He remained standing there like a great big Christmas lumberjack, and she decided to pace because it was a sore subject for her.

"The concept of virginity is so old fashioned, I know that," she said. "I mean, technically, I can say I 'lost' my virginity to a heavy flow tampon when I was thirteen because I didn't buy a junior size."

He nodded along, despite the knot of confusion when she said *tampon*, and let her talk.

"My family is pretty traditional. School, marriage, kids. My mom and grandma always warned us to 'save' ourselves for marriage, and I was always a good little girl, so I listened. Helena was the rebellious one and had a party celebrating the end of her virginity, which almost gave our father a stroke when he found out. And Gracie's first time was more of an experiment and very clinical."

"But not you," Alexander offered, grinning far too much for her level of anxiety.

"By the time I realized that I didn't want to wait, I'd sat through one of those horrible Sex Ed videos about STDs during health class."

"Pardon?"

Lia couldn't believe she was explaining sexually transmitted diseases, but there she was. "Don't you have them?"

Alexander laughed deep from his belly. "Not personally. Besides, we don't have disease in the Eternal Winter Forest."

"Right, paradise should be STD free." She drank and felt her cheeks flush even more from the whisky. "*Anyway*, it's not like I didn't try. In college I went on a few dates with a guy I really liked, and we went back to his dorm, but I got my period early, and he was so freaked out."

"By blood?" Alexander exclaimed. "He sounds weak."

"I've tried a few times since then. Once, I snapped the condom on my date's dick so hard it broke the skin, and we went to the emergency room. Another time, I was dating this guy, and I discovered he didn't shower. He only used baby wipes. I've been told I'm too picky, too prudish, too whatever. But I think I want something simple."

Alexander made a noise of understanding. His voice came out low when he said, "And what do you want, Lia?"

Crawl to me.

"I want...to be *wanted*. I want to feel good." Her eyes fluttered closed, and the first thing, the *very first thing*, she thought of was Alexander washing her in the tub. "On my terms. With someone who respects me."

"And what about the love you crave?" he asked her, face to face, his breath sweet with whisky.

"I've given up having it all." She smiled sadly. "But when it comes to sex, I know now that I want it to be you."

She didn't know what she was going to say until she said it.

He made a sound, half torture, half moan. "You do not know what you ask, Lia."

She bounced on the tips of her toes, too nervous to stand still. She didn't know how to be sexy and seductive like she'd seen in movies and read in books. She only knew how to be herself, for better or for worse.

She didn't make it a habit of throwing herself at anyone, especially not winter gods descended from saints. Usually, her desires were buried under layers of fear, overthinking, and carefully planned lists. She'd constructed a tower of insecurities over thirty plus years of the world chipping away at her. But in their cabin, in the kitchen, warm with roasting meat and smokey whisky, the world couldn't reach her.

When he didn't respond, she puffed a sigh and put their empty teacups on the kitchen counter. The moment she brushed past him, he grabbed her free wrist and squeezed. The pressure was surprising. Her eyelids fluttered. Her pulse point hummed like wings under his touch. He brought himself up to his full height, walking her back until her ass hit the side of the kitchen table.

"Are you certain?"

She nodded.

"Because I do want you. I want to make you feel good, Lia. I've admired you since the moment I saw how hard you fought to live."

Lia couldn't breathe at his words. He checked all her boxes, and more. "I'm certain. I want it to be you."

"What do you want from me?" His voice was demanding. "I need you to say it."

"I—" She wanted so many things all at once. She wanted his mouth all over. Wanted to feel his cock. Wanted everything she'd denied herself for years because it hadn't been *right*. Because it hadn't been what she *needed*. Now she knew exactly what she needed, and he was there and willing and so beautiful it hurt to look at him.

"Kiss me," she said, and swiftly added, "please."

And Alexander, runaway king, son of saints, gave her exactly what she asked for.

🦋 10 🦋

ALEXANDER

Alexander gathered Lia by her hips and set her on the kitchen table. He wanted to commit her to memory, because even though he was the one from a faraway realm, she was the one who felt too good to be real.

He cradled her face, admiring the round sweep of her cheekbones, the long lashes casting shadows over her constellation of beauty marks. The most divine part of her in that moment was the swollen bottom lip she'd been biting all day long. Even in the most intimate bath of his life, he'd still wanted her mouth first.

Alexander pressed his lips to hers. He nearly whimpered at how soft she felt. How kissing her was like a release, an undoing of the fear that had been following him since he'd run. They fit perfectly, and he pressed harder just because he loved the little moans she made when he did.

He parted her mouth with his tongue, and she met him with urgency. She tasted like sugar and smoke from the drink, and he thought he could survive on just her kisses for as long as she'd let him. The thought startled him, but he only pulled back long enough to see the sexy flutter of her long lashes and a smile that gutted him.

"Kiss me again," she whispered.

He cupped the back of her neck, and she scooted to the edge of the table, trapping him with her thighs. He palmed her lower back to bring her closer still. She moaned louder as he ground his stiff, aching cock against her mound.

How had no one in their right mind ever kissed her good and proper? Lia, with a mouth he would have pledged his sword to. Him, the broken knight, the never-king in voluntary exile. He knew in his wretched heart that he didn't deserve her. She was everything bright and hopeful and *good*. He was nothing but ruin. The thing he should have been doing was keeping her safe, getting her back to her family, not taking pleasure in the way she looked at him. A better man would have denied her, let her find someone better suited for her, someone who could give her the world she wanted instead of the shame in his heart. But he was not a better man. He was weak, and he would give her everything she asked.

He deepened his kisses, nipping at her delicious plump lips, swollen pink. He grabbed her by her chin. "This is my lip, do you understand?"

"Yes, yours." She ran her fingers over his heart. He wanted to press her palm there. Ask her to listen to the way it beat faster for her.

But then she trailed it down to his cock, ringing the outline of the shaft against his thigh.

"I want more," she whispered at her ear, guiding his hand between her legs. She was soaked through the fabric. So wet his legs nearly gave out from under him at the thought of slipping into her tight, silky heat. "Please."

Did she know that single word from her was enough to undo him? He had to be strong. He couldn't fuck a virgin this way. He needed to prepare her to take him. To give her the control she wanted.

"All in time, my greedy little darling," he said, his voice gravelly with desire. "Lie back."

She did as he asked. Her hair spilled in black waves against the scuffed oak table. She arched her back like she couldn't take not being touched even for a moment. He squeezed her thighs and hooked the waistband, tugging the trousers down and over the curves of her hips, past her muscular calves. He discarded the burdensome clothes on the floor.

"I—" she said, squeezing her knees together. To hide her most secret place from him. "No one has ever kissed me there."

"Does it make you nervous?" He palmed her belly to keep her still, keep her from squirming.

She bit her finger and nodded. Saints, she was so perfect.

He kissed her closed knees one by one. "What can I do to make you trust me?"

"I do trust you."

You shouldn't, was his first thought. But he knew he wanted to earn that trust. He might not have been the son his father had wanted, or the king his people needed, but he could give this beautiful woman pleasure.

"Then let me see you your sweet cunt. Let me make you feel good, Lia."

She gasped at his words then spread her legs open. He got on his knees and buried his face against the damp cotton that still covered her. He ran a tongue between her seam and waited for her to wriggle, to get used to his touch, to the invasion of his nose pressing against the berry of her clitoris.

When she fisted his hair and tugged and asked for more, more, he removed her underwear and added it to the pile. She propped herself up on her elbows and her felt the unfamiliar urge to preen like a fucking peacock at the way she looked at him. Her cheeks were flushed and her lips were parted, releasing fast little gasps.

"Can you take your clothes off?" she asked.

"As you wish, darling." He grinned as he tugged off his sweater. Undid the top button of his trousers. His cock strained against the enclosure and wanted release. But he wouldn't have it. Not yet. He stopped and chuckled at Lia's disappointed pout.

"I wish that. You said you'd have sex with me." Her little whine was adorable, and he fell back to his knees. "Shouldn't you be naked?"

"I said..." He kissed the tender skin of her inner thighs. "That I would make you feel good. Now, tell me how you feel?"

She whimpered a little but then smiled. There it was. The sheer vulnerable joy on her face twisted something new inside of him.

"I feel like a bottle of champagne," she said. "Like someone shook me and I need to..."

"Pop?" he offered, breathing in her clean, sweet smell.

"Mmhmm."

"Then let me drink you, darling."

Her dusky folds glistened, and he felt like a starving man as he dragged his tongue between them. She gasped and lightly lifted her hips. He closed his mouth over her pink, stiff clit and licked her hard and slow, until she melted against him. Until she breathed his name in long, luxurious cries.

He penetrated her with his tongue. Devouring her wetness. Kissing and sucking and letting her grind her pussy on his face as much as she wanted and needed. He wanted to be there for her to use. For her pleasure, as long as she desired. To grant the wishes she longed for. And when she bucked against his mouth, she squeezed her thighs against his ears, and it was like listening to the crash of wave after wave. He wanted to drown in those waves, inside her.

When she went languid and breathed a pretty sigh, he caressed the insides of her thighs, kissed his way up her trim brown curls.

"Alexander?" she asked, her voice too strained. She should have been languid and sated.

He stood, fearing that he might have inadvertently hurt her. Then he felt it, the burn running up his forearm. Swift black swirls, the singular patterns of snow crystals and vines.

How? He hadn't used his power, not willingly. He scanned her body, but all he had to do was look up to find the ceiling blanketed in dozens, hundreds of twinkling stars.

❧ II ❧
LIA

At first, Lia thought the sudden bursts of light were behind her eyes. Alexander had made her feel so good, and she'd never come with another person before. But when her orgasm finished settling all over her body, and she blinked, she knew she very much *wasn't* imagining the colorful lights drifting down from the ceiling. A marbled glow of greens, purples, and gold danced over their skin. It was truly one of the most beautiful things she'd ever seen, next to Alexander.

"It certainly brings new meaning to fireworks." She giggled playfully, then registered how still Alexander was. "What's wrong?"

The dark marks of his tattoo were spreading, a trail of sparks cutting across his skin. His face was twisted with pain and uncertainty, and she felt a pull deep within her because she didn't want him to hurt. She wanted him to feel as good as she did.

"Alexander?" she asked again.

Naked from the waist down, Lia sat up. Should she go to him? She wished she could ask her sisters what you were supposed to do in the event the person who'd made you come seems to be having a supernatural freak out. Somehow, she thought that neither Helena nor Gracie could help her. It was a whole new world, and she had to adapt.

"*Alexander*," she said once more, sharper. "What happened?"

This time, he leveled his golden eyes with hers. The deep furrows of his brow knit together. He seemed to come back to himself. He licked his lips, and she couldn't help but think that he was still tasting her.

Get a grip, she scolded herself. But she already knew she couldn't get enough of him.

"I cannot say, Lia," he told her. "I've never seen my brother or father do anything like this."

"Do you use magic when you—" For God's sake. If she couldn't say *cunnilingus* out loud then she shouldn't be having it.

Alexander seemed to catch what she was getting at and scoffed. He stalked back toward her, and this time she paid no attention to the light phenomenon he'd conjured. All she could see was the heat in his eyes and the hard rod straining against the leg of his trousers. Her fingers itched to undo those buttons, to finish what they had started.

"My talents are hard earned, darling," he said in a low growl. "And yet..."

His thighs pressed at the crossed barrier of her knees. It would be so easy to open up for him again. She wanted to. But she also recognized the turmoil within him and urged him on.

"And yet?" Lia asked.

"There was a moment between us when I wanted to show you everything. Including the clash of angels."

The tiny bursts of light drifted down, and for a moment it was as if they were inside a snow globe made of stars. She extended her hand, and the first of the light bursts touched the pad of her index finger. It tickled, and she imagined this was as close as she would get to being kissed by the sun. Alexander had made this because of her, and he hadn't even intended on it. A tiny thrill ran through her knowing that she had made this strong, beautiful winter god lose control.

"Oh, Alexander," she said, guilt working its way under her skin. "Your mark...I'm sorry."

He grabbed hold of her chin, forcing their eyes to meet. His frown deepened, and there was something so earnest in his amber eyes, she felt frozen by them. "It's not your fault, darling Lia. I am not in control of these powers. But it ends tonight with the solstice moon. I will be rid of this curse—and then—I suppose I didn't plan that far."

When Alexander released her, Lia found herself leaning forward, missing his touch. He walked away, opening a series of drawers until he found a linen cloth. He ran it under the faucet and returned to her.

Her heart slammed in her throat as she accepted it. The heir of Saint Nikolas had brought her a wet towel. Her sisters would never let her forget it. *If* they believed her in the first place. Lia barely believed it herself.

"Alexander," she said, slipping back into her wool leggings. She'd abandoned the ridiculous sense of shame somewhere between the bath and her orgasm. No, even before that, when she'd woken up from the nightmare of almost drowning. Shame had no place here, in their secluded world of magic and stars.

"Noelia," he responded, opening the oven to baste the turkey as her stomach made ill-timed hungry noises.

"You've brought me back from the brink of death. You've healed my wound. You *created* all of this—" She gestured to the drifting lights that fell on every surface and vanished.

He made a short, grunting sound as he shut the oven. "Yes?"

"Why do you insist on calling it a curse?"

"Because it *is*." Alexander swallowed hard and kept his back turned to her, bare shoulders tense. "There are things I've seen my father do. Things I've done."

"You are not your father, Alex." She didn't know how to comfort him, only rested her hand on his shoulder and watched as the tension eased from him as he slowly turned to face her. Deep down, she knew that there was something he wasn't telling her, but whatever it was, Alexander needed to trust her enough to get there on his own.

"And now I never will be." Alexander trembled under her touch. For a moment he looked both lost and relieved. It was a look she recognized in herself. "This mark was the only thing my father ever loved. I only wish he could witness me end his line."

As the conjured light bursts began to fall faster and dissipate, the house gave a mild shudder. The plates and teacups in the open cabinets rattled. Wilted potted plants strung against the far window swung like a pendulum.

She was just about to ask what was happening when the kitchen door swung and swung like a pendulum. She looked to Alexander, but she could already see the source of the disturbance. The marks were spreading again, this time burning their way up to his forearms.

"Is that you?"

"I'm not—" A hard clatter and crash interrupted him.

They ran into the living room where they found the window shutters and front door had slammed open. The wind that came through pushed her back so hard, Lia would have been lifted off her feet if Alexander hadn't grabbed her waist.

"I don't know how to make it stop!" he shouted as the Mark of the Saint ran up his biceps like a living matchstick. His eyes shimmering gold, ethereal melted metal. Veins raised at the sides of his throat as he fought with the living power overtaking him.

Lia did not know anything about magical realms and saints that were more than legends. But she did know what it was like to feel your life was not in your control. She could feel the fear that made him tremble as he held her.

And so, Lia Espinoza did the only thing she could think of. She pushed herself on the tips of her toes and kissed him. She felt the syncopated rhythm of his heart as she snaked her palms over his hard chest. He exhaled softly against Lia, pinning her to him as he kissed her back. The snowy breeze curled inside, tracking in heaps of snow that nearly reached the height of the door. Lia was distantly aware that the flames in the fireplace had doubled in height, scorching the snow into puddles on contact.

None of it mattered as Alexander walked her back and pressed her against the wall. Something fell at their side, but neither looked down. All they could feel was each other. Her soft places against the hard planes of him. Alexander's lips were firm, his expert tongue searching for hers. She met him with a fervor that surprised her.

Lia was already breathless, and this time it was her turn to lose control. To feel like her body was not her own. To burn with so much want that it would reduce her to cinders.

Before that moment, Lia had experienced a handful of perfunctory but underwhelming kisses. She hadn't known what she wanted then. She hadn't known how to ask for the type of kiss she *needed*. Worse, how could she ever have anything but this type of kiss? Alexander and his full mouth and wicked tongue. Alexander and his intensity that struck her like she was the steel to his flint.

When he pulled back, panting, it was because the storm of ice and fire around them had stopped. Snowflakes were suspended in the air. The wind had died, but snow still drifted into the threshold and windows. Most importantly, Alexander's tattoo had stopped spreading.

He turned to her with glassy, golden eyes full of fierce emotion. "How did you know that would work?"

"I didn't," she answered honestly, her pulse heavy in her ears, at her throat, even at the center of her swollen lips. "I've been overwhelmed before. When it happens, I've trained myself to focus. That's why I started making lists. I figured you could focus on me."

"What if I'd hurt you?" he asked softly, though he rested his palm at the crook of her throat, inching his touch up to cup her face. Traced the delicate scar on her chin.

She gazed down at him, brushing a lock of hair away from his eyes. "You wouldn't have."

The corners of his lips twitched with a reluctant smile, then Alexander turned to examine the damage. The fireplace had burned scorch marks a couple of feet across the brick floor and mantel. Even the chin of the polar bear. A river of melted snow had begun to freeze with the chill coming in through the open windows and doors.

He examined the swirls of ivy and strange runes had stopped at the swell of his biceps. "My brother walked around the palace practicing the words he'd say when it was his turn. He was born to it. I never even paid attention to the Helleböne Priestesses when they talked about the winter solstice or when the moon would be in place."

"I can help with that," she said, and found her phone. The battery was preserving well on airplane mode. Lia pulled up the world calendar app that had even the most obscure holidays. She held up the phone to him, the image with snow-capped pines that read 8:19 P.M. "We have six hours."

"Six hours," he repeated, then held her phone up and down, side to side, like he was expecting there to be a witch inside of it.

"I *wonder* what we can do in six hours," Lia said, tugging her lower lip between her teeth.

Alexander watched her with rekindled desire, and something else. Something that hadn't been there when he'd held her in the bath or spread her legs to eat her pussy. It was fear.

"I don't want to hurt you, Lia," he said. "I don't have control of these powers."

She couldn't help the disappointment that colored her features. "I thought you were a man of your word."

"Perhaps you'll finally believe me when I say that I am not a good man, and certainly not worthy of you."

Lia refused to believe that, but she couldn't make that decision for him.

"But tonight," he continued, his voice low and heavy with desire. "After the solstice, when I can no longer be crowned king and saint, when I end the line of my forefathers, I will make you mine, Lia Espinoza. And that is the only promise a rake and dishonorable prince can make you."

His words sang along her skin. Lia had waited decades to have sex. How hard could another six hours be?

12

ALEXANDER

Six hours. That's how long Alexander had to wait before he was free. Six hours until he could take sweet Lia and fill her perfect, silky cunt with his cock. He throbbed at the thought of her.

Six hours.

He could make it. He wasn't an animal, after all. Though, revelers of the Hellebörne orgies might say differently.

He rummaged through the Guardian's supplies and found a hammer and a box of nails. He nailed the shutters closed and bolted the door in the event he lost control again. All the while, Lia mopped up the melted snow. Out of the corner of his eye, he kept a close watch on her. Alexander couldn't understand how this human, with her anxious, exuberant energy and big laughter, had broken him out of his reverie.

Truthfully, he didn't know how he'd lost his grip on his powers. Though, if he were *truly* honest, he would have admitted that he'd never had a grip on them to begin with. The first time he'd used them, it had been to break through the ice. Then, he'd filled Lia with warmth to bring her back from the clutches of death. He'd healed the shadow sylph poison from her wound. He'd conjured a vision of starlight because he'd wanted to give her everything, more than just his mouth and tongue.

Alexander knew that as the spare heir of the Nikolas, he possessed the dregs of power. With that power, he'd honed himself into living pleasure. But he'd never experienced the things he'd shared with Lia. As he shuttered the windows and hammered the final nails, he remembered the snow that had hung suspended in mid-air. Lia had picked up a flake on her finger and brought it to her tongue.

Oh, how he wanted to be reduced to a fucking bit of ice just to be touched by her.

She glanced up and gave him one of those sweet, impossible smiles. The kind that made him believe perhaps, just perhaps, he was worthy. If not of his kingdom, then of her.

But when he pictured her bent over his lap, his palm soothing the red handprints he wanted to leave on her generous rump, Alexander knew he'd never be more than a rake, useful for only one thing.

"I'm going to wash up before dinner," she told him, holding up her soot-covered hands.

He made an unintelligible sound because he remembered how trusting, how gentle she'd been with him in the bath. No one had touched him the way Lia had. Knowing that no one ever would again brought a strange, unfamiliar sensation to the pit of his stomach. After they survived the snowstorm, he'd reunite her with her sisters, and then he'd keep going in his search for his new life. Though, he hadn't given much thought to where his new life would be and how it would look like. Instead, he was back up against the wall, devouring Lia's supple mouth. He was on the kitchen table eating her cunt. He was soothing her in the bath.

Alexander needed to busy himself because his thoughts

only returned to the painful erection in his pants. He found another sweater.

"Curse you, Elowen," he grumbled as he pulled it on. It was a soft wool, deep red, with moth holes at the seams of the armpits.

Then, when he thought of Elowen, the Guardian of the Path, the dweller of the cabin, and he felt that heavy pressure in his heart. He'd left her. He'd left the kingdom. But his last living brother was strong, cunning, downright manipulative. If anyone could take back the kingdom, it was Hans.

When the fireplace burned a little too hot and he felt another tremble, Alexander knew his trigger was too much emotion. Fear, terror, desperation.

But not when Lia had kissed him. She'd been his anchor in his own personal storm. He considered running up the stairs to beg her to kiss him. Touch him. Do what she wanted with him. Use her strange power to comfort him because his mind was possibly breaking after moments without her.

How could be make it until nightfall?

How could he make it a lifetime?

He balled his hands into fists and braced himself. If he was going to fuck her properly, he needed to be in control of his body and mind. She was trusting him with her pleasure, and he had to be better.

Prepare.

He righted anything his burst of power had upturned. He cleaned every inch of the living room, even fluffing the fucking pillows. When he was done he made his way to the kitchen. He stepped on something sharp that shot a prick of pain up his leg. It was a tiny square of wood. Like a tooth. No, a roof shingle from a toy house. Elowen's cuckoo clock had landed in a dark corner. They must have knocked it over when they'd kissed against the wall.

He was harder than ever at the memory of it. The clock had broken in their burst of passion, and its miniature doors were stuck, with the tiny bird wedged half-way out. He hung it back in place, then finally returned to the kitchen to set the table. None of the place settings or porcelain plates or glasses matched because there had been generations of Guardians who had lived in the cabin, but he found the best ones without chips or cracks for him and Lia.

He removed the turkey from the oven and set it to rest the way the palace cooks had taught him. He rummaged through Elowen's cache of bottles, the only thing that there was a surplus of in the cabin, and opened another bottle of red wine at the center of the table.

Just when he was finished lighting the long taper candles all along the windows and kitchen counter, he heard the wheeze of the pipes, and a small, almost whisper of a moan. He was still, so utterly still he could have been a tree in a forest. There it was again. That moan, sharper that before.

"Fuck," he hissed, gripping the counter. "Fuck."

Unless there was a third person in the cabin with them, Lia was pleasuring herself. Touching herself in the place where he deeply wanted to be.

The acoustics of the pipes rattled down her pretty sounds. They haunted him until he was undoing his trousers with shaking fingers and taking hold of his cock, so hard it was nearly painful. He leaned against the kitchen counter and spilled cooking oil on his hand, then roughly pumped his fist up and down his shaft. His shallow breaths matched the rapid cadence of Lia's moans. She was close. So was he.

A thrilling sensation shot to his groin when he realized that she hadn't made it through the six hours either. That she was hot and needy. That perhaps she had rushed upstairs to rub her pulsing little berry and everything else was pretense.

"Fuck," he grunted as he squeezed his own base. Fucked his own hand. Fucked the very air, desperately wanting inside Lia. But he couldn't because he was afraid of hurting her with his cursed power. It was that thought that struck through him, centered him. Focused his perverted act and listened to the breathy sighs that echoed down to him until he knew she had finished.

It took all his self-control, but he stopped himself. His balls were heavy and drawn up tightly to the heat of his aching body. But he didn't want to spill. Couldn't spill without her again. He needed to give her everything he had, and now, he was ready.

He buttoned up his trousers, washed his hands, and sat down at the table to pour himself a glass of wine.

Moments later, Lia appeared through those doors dressed in a creamy tunic cinched by a leather strap he was certain was one of Elowen's suspenders. Her hair fell in raven waves around her face, glowing and golden in the candlelight.

His entire body wanted to lurch forward. To touch her. Hold her. Kiss her. Thank her for simply being with him, even if it was because they were trapped in the snow. Even if it was for a breath in the span of their lives.

"Hey," she said.

"Hello." He stood and bowed before her.

She touched the corners of her tunic and genuflected. It was clumsy and adorable, and his heart felt like it was in a vise because she was still too far away.

"Alex, this is amazing." She turned in a circle, taking in the candles and table. Then she returned to him and beamed. "Now let's eat because I'm starving."

"Come darling," he said. "I'm ravenous."

She tried to hide her blush with a purse of her lips. She found the sharpest knife and carved the turkey. "I'll plate, since you did all this."

He eased back into his chair and touched his finger to the taper candle, enjoying the way the hot wax warmed his finger. "Tell me about your other lists, Lia."

She looked up from slicing through the tendons of the turkey leg and smiled so widely, he had that feeling again, like someone had a grip around his heart. What was wrong with his insides? He drank, as if that was the cure for everything. But in the back of his thoughts, he knew that she, *she* was the cure for whatever ailed him. He simply wasn't ready to admit it.

"Which ones?"

"The ones you say are in your magic mirror."

"It's a smart phone," she corrected, ripping a piece of flesh and savoring it.

As she returned to the table with their dishes, neither of them waited for the other to dive in. They each had a drumstick, potatoes that were charred at the edges, and root vegetables that still sizzled. They ate with their fingers, holding on to the drumstick bone and licking the salty juice from their fingertips.

"I'm sorry," she apologized with a laughing bark. "I usually have better table manners."

"Never," he said. Alexander had already conjured a thousand images of Lia eating him instead of that bloody bird. "Now, the lists."

"I already read you one."

Alexander leaned forward on his elbows and grinned. "Ah, yes, but that was before you confessed there are more. I'd like to hear them."

She rolled her eyes, taking a long sip from her wine. She seemed more languid, and his cock gave a hard jolt at the memory of her moans.

"Fine. But you can't laugh," Lia said. She tapped the screen of her magic mirror and dragger her finger across rapidly. The things she could do with those fingers... "Top five movies, though you probably don't have movies in Santa's Workshop."

"The *Eternal* Winter Kingdom," he corrected, not that he should care anymore.

"Top ten subway stations," she said, "I feel like we should ease into the New York part of your human education. Ah, here we are. Top five rock ballads. You do have music where you're from?"

"*Of course* we have music." Alexander scoffed. "Galiel's symphonies always pack the amphitheater during the summer."

He didn't know why that made her laugh so much, but it was worth it. She proceeded to list songs.

"'Stairway to Heaven,'" she said, "Has the best guitar riffs. It is the length of two songs, but I always play it when I want to feel dramatic."

"Play it for me," he said. "Can you?"

She tapped her magic mirror again. "I have to conserve phone battery so that I can message my sisters. So, I'll play my top *top* song."

An uneasy sensation overcame him at the thought of leaving her again, but he still raised his wine. "Go on, then."

"Number four is 'Sweet Child O' Mine' by Guns N' Roses, which I prefer over 'November Rain.'"

"Is 'November Rain' number three?"

She crunched her nose and shook her head. So incandescent was she that he didn't dare interrupt her anymore. He loved that she made anything sound special, even a list of her favorite songs. When had he cared enough about something to remember it?

"Number three is 'Have You Ever Seen the Rain' by Creedence Clearwater Revival. Hands down. Number two is 'Iris' by the Goo Goo Dolls."

"Dare I ask you for your number one?" he asked.

"Well..." She leaned in like she was keeping a secret. "It's a tie between Heart's 'What About Love?' and 'Dreams' by Fleetwood Mac."

"Let's hear both then." And when the songs filtered out of her strange magical contraption, he felt he was seeing her for the very first time because these were things that she loved, and she was sharing them with him.

"My sisters don't like them," she said, resting her chin on her fists. "We're so different. I used to wonder how we were related. But deep down we want the same things. Happiness. Family. Love."

Things I can't give you, he thought.

The Christmas prince unceremoniously took a bite of the drumstick and chewed for a long time before washing it down with a big gulp of wine.

"We have very different families," he said darkly.

"Tell me." Her words were so soft, they dragged him out of the wretched, resentful place he usually kept memories of his brothers.

And he would tell her because she asked, because he wouldn't deny her. "When my brother Wilhelm was born, there was a celebration. The would-be king. He was even *born* on the solstice. Tonight would have been his fortieth birthday."

Lia sat forward, tangling her fingers between his, and when he held her, he felt stronger.

"When my second brother was born," Alexander continued, "the kingdom celebrated again. Here was the future Master of Alchemy, crowned with the golden laurels that marked his place as the heir who kept the kingdom in riches and secrets of the throne.

"And when I was born, my mother grew ill and not even the Nikolas, the bloody Saint with his God-given powers, could save her life. And so, there were no parades, no celebrations.

When I was born, there was only mourning. Even my brothers kept a distance, and so I grew up running wild for a time, shattering windows in the palace with Kit—"

Alexander stopped, startled at his own story, and a name he hadn't spoken out loud in over twenty years.

"Who is Kit?" she asked.

"He *was* my cousin." He cleared his throat. "So, you see, our families are very different. At least, I hope your father has never told you that you are expendable."

"You're not expendable," Lia said, squeezing his hand, and he held on because that was all he could do. His anchor in his personal storm.

"You don't know me."

Lia shrugged. "I want to know you."

He didn't deserve her. He didn't deserve her calm or the adoration in her deep, dark eyes. He wanted to save her from him, and so he said, "Do you know what I was doing when my brother was being murdered?"

Lia gave a confused shake of her head, brushing her thumb over his. "Whatever it is—"

"I had my cock buried in a pretty maiden. I don't remember her name. She got me off under the table where my brother was giving his very final speech, not that any of us knew it at the time. And even though I knew people suspected what we were doing, I didn't stop her. I let her tug me till release and then stole her into a private chamber and fucked every part of her that she would let me because I wanted to be anywhere, anywhere except at my brother's side."

Lia swallowed hard. She touched the crescent moon between her clavicles, and Alexander had the urge to press his mouth there, to feel how hard her heart must be hammering at his crude words. He wanted her to revile him, because every memory—the feast, their births—all of it brought him too close to the things he wanted to forget. How could she still want him after that?

"Are they—" she began, and he could see her courage, building like a long snowfall. "Are they the same things you're going to do to me?"

"*Saints*, Lia," he gritted between his teeth. "I'm trying to tell you that I am not right for you. Innocent and good."

"What if I don't want to be innocent and good?"

He stared at her, then. She was unearthly, gilded in candle-flame and the warmth of the kitchen. There was a moment when he forgot how much he hated his own past. All he could think of were the songs she'd played for him and her laughter and kiss that had tamed his wild, wretched heart.

In that moment, he wanted Lia and only Lia, even if he did not deserve her. A better man would have turned her away. Been stronger. But he was not a better man.

He meant to tell her so, but then there was a terrible sound. Horns and harps louder than he was prepared for.

She tapped the screen of her magic mirror, and a devilish smile transformed her beautiful face. "It's eight nineteen, Alexander. It's the solstice."

Neither of them breathed for a moment. Alexander reached out to the candle flame, in his mind imagining that it would grow tall, like the fireplace earlier in the day. Nothing happened. He rucked up the sleeves of his sweater, but the Mark of the Saint didn't move. It didn't melt away either. And yet, when he tried to summon the sparks of light, when he searched for the foreign power in his veins, nothing happened. Nothing.

"It's over," Alexander said, nearly breathless. "It's over."

"It's over," she repeated.

He shot to his feet and grabbed a bottle of sparkling wine. He cupped the cold base in one hand and picked up a blade in the other. In a swift swipe of the knife, he sabered the head of the frothy wine and tipped the contents into his mouth. The fizzy liquid was cool and bright against his tongue.

He turned around to share the bottle with Lia, but her hands were occupied as she undid the leather cinching her waist.

"You have a promise to keep, Alexander," she said.

His cruel fate might have been over, but his night with Lia had just begun.

❧ 13 ☙
LIA

The thing about being an accidental thirty-three-year-old virgin was that Lia spent too much time building it up. Every time she'd gotten close, the event had turned into a disaster. Earlier that day, she'd been so wound up, she'd made herself come just to take pressure off the very thing she was asking Alexander to do.

Though he'd already made her orgasm with his mouth, she didn't want to get so much in her head that it would be another spectacular disappointment. She hated that she felt that way, that other men had made her feel like there was something wrong with her because she wasn't as confident as Helena or as adventurous as Gracie. She'd always imagined she'd meet a sensitive, hot, bookish man who adored her. She'd imagined they'd have dinner, stroll through the shelves of the Strand, and then return to her place where she'd wear something with lace. It was one of the many fantasies Lia had conjured.

Now, Lia was miles from everything familiar. A cabin in the woods with a runaway winter god hadn't been in her fantasies, but now it was as if it had only ever been him. The compass inside her heart, perhaps the very thing that had led her to the

Black Forest, was pointing at the devastatingly handsome man holding a sabered bottle of champagne and staring at her like she was prey in the forest.

Without a doubt, Lia knew that it had to be Alexander. Alexander with his brooding, pouty mouth and molten gold eyes. Alexander who protected her and kissed her like she was a morsel to be devoured. Alexander who lit her up from within like a Christmas tree.

"Lia," he growled her name.

Her pulse raced, and she felt it everywhere—her throat, her fingertips, her clit. Every part of her thrummed with anticipation. She went through the doors, tossing her linen shirt over her shoulder. Then her leggings. Her panties. She wanted to undress herself, to leave her clothes like breadcrumbs up the stairs and into the small bedroom. She stood at the foot of the bed, trembling with the newness of her desire, her defiant confidence that seemed to bloom like a desert rose because Lia Espinoza did not lead men into candlelit bedrooms and Lia Espinoza did not strip tease and Lia Espinoza did not run away.

Fuck it.

As it turned out, Lia Espinoza *did*. She was tired of being expected to be one thing. Of being *expected*. She longed to be reckless.

Alexander peeled off his sweater. His broad, muscular chest rose and fell quickly, and knowing that he was just as eager made her close the short distance between them. She tugged at his waistband, running a hand up his rock-hard shaft.

A tiny moan escaped her then, and he chuckled darkly as she worked the buttons of his trousers with shaky fingers.

"Let me," he said.

"I want to." She steadied herself, cursing his kingdom for not having zippers. "I want every part of this, not just the sex."

When she was finished, agonizing seconds later, she tugged the fabric down his powerful thighs, dusted with dark hair.

Lia had seen dicks before. She'd watched porn to stimulate herself, and she'd taken biology courses, and she'd *almost* had sex several times. But nothing, absolutely nothing, had prepared her for Alexander's cock.

"It's so—" she said, searching for the right word. Being naked with someone while talking about their body parts felt like letting them touch a bruise.

Alexander only *laughed*. Low, amused, pleased. "I know, darling."

She fought the urge to roll her eyes, but she couldn't fault him for being so arrogant. It was big. Really big. Thick and the color of a dusty rose. His head flared pink and beaded with the liquid crystal of his semen. The shadow of green veins traced his length, and wetness pooled between her legs at the thought of having all of that inside her. Would it hurt? Did she *want* it to hurt?

She sat at the foot of the bed to get a better look at it. "Can I touch you now?"

He held her gaze and guided her hand to his base.

"Oh," she gasped and watched his eyes flutter as she closed her fist around him. Or tried. "I think my hand is too small."

"Or my cock is too big, sunshine."

"You sure flatter yourself."

He smiled hard, closing his fist around hers and guiding her into slow, long strokes until she picked up the rhythm he liked on her own. She stacked her right hand on top of the left and twisted, dragging her thumb over his wet tip.

When he hissed, she stopped. "Does that hurt?"

"Don't stop, Lia," he said, every muscle in his long body flexed with desire. He thrust up into her hands, and she resumed touching him. She grazed his balls and saw the way they constricted at the base. A vein snaked from the dark trail of hair across his abdomen, and she leaned forward to kiss it, never stopping the movement of her hands. He smelled earthy, clean, and a bit of the smoke that clung to him from tending to the fireplace. She was so curious about what made him sigh and groan. She was amazed at how he could look so much like he was in pain, but still wanted her to keep going. Everything about Alexander fascinated her, and she wanted to be such a good girl for him.

She tightened her grip on his shaft, stroking in fast little pumps. She kissed the tip of him, running her tongue at edge of his frenulum in broad strokes. That's when his knees nearly buckled.

"*Fuck*, I'm going to come," he growled and fisted her hair. He tilted her head back, exposing her neck. He took his cock roughly into his own fist and pumped hard.

She traced a line across the tops of her small breasts, encircling the hard buds of her nipples. "Come on me. Right here."

His amber eyes burned, and she thought she saw a real spark there, like the *hiss* of a match. Then, warm, wet semen spilled across her chest and dripped, glistening, down her breasts.

The act felt filthy. She wanted more. She squeezed her thighs, rubbing them together to try and sate the heavy feeling building there.

"Alexander," Lia said. "I need you now."

"Tell me, sunshine. Tell me where it aches." He sank to his knees in front of her. He kissed the tops of her thighs. The strong muscles of her calves, carved by years of running track.

She eased back onto her elbows, the plush mattress enveloping her weight. She uncrossed her legs. Let her knees fall to the side. Never in her whole life had she thought she'd be brave enough to touch herself in front of someone else, but she dragged her own fingers through her wet seam and around her clitoris.

"Look at what you do to me, Lia," he said, shuddering as his cock twitched. "I'm so hard again."

She let her head drop back and said, "And look at what you do to me."

"I want you to fuck yourself," he told her. Wedging his legs between hers, standing there with his cock in hand, masturbating over her. "Fuck yourself with your fingers like you did earlier. That's right. I fucking heard you."

She gasped. "You heard me?"

Alexander grunted as he watched her slip one finger in, then rock against her palm. "Every little moan and sigh. You couldn't wait, could you?"

A bright shock of pleasure started at her clitoris and she felt like she was digging and digging to unearth that delicious rush that came with sex. "No, I couldn't. I wanted you so much."

"Did you think of me?"

"Y-yes," she shivered. "I wanted it to be your fingers, your mouth. Your cock." She met his eyes and held his stare. Her skin was on fire. He'd heard her. He'd heard her masturbating before dinner. Instead of shame, she felt a thrill because the way he looked at her, it meant he liked it. "Did you do this while you listened?"

"I fucked my own hand thinking of you. Thinking of filling your virgin cunt with my cock."

"I want you now, Alexander," she said, breathless. "I feel empty without it. *Please*."

"Know this, Lia. Know that this is the last time you're going to feel this way. Because after I'm inside of you, you're never going to feel as full as when my cock is in your cunt. Do you understand that?"

The way he spoke those words broke something inside her.

She was steel made pliable, molten so she could be reshaped into something stronger.

"Please, Alex. I want to be yours. Make me yours."

He grabbed the hand she used to pleasure herself and brought her wet fingers to his mouth. He sucked them clean, holding her wrist with a possessive ferocity that made her wetter still.

"I—I want my first time to be on top," she said.

"My body is yours, Lia." He climbed up on the bed, resting on the midnight blue velvet pillows.

She took in every part of him. The regal features of his face made jagged from a lifetime of fighting. His strong body and proud cock he slowly stroked as he watched her straddle his waist.

"Take your time, darling," he said, his voice deep and soothing. "I'm not going anywhere."

At the back of her mind she thought, *yes you are.* But that was a problem for the morning.

With her knees on either side of him, Lia was open, exposed. She positioned her wet seam on his thick, beautiful penis. She rocked back and forth, gliding it between her labia as she rested her hands on his abdomen for support.

"Oh God, I could come just from this."

He raised his hips, and another spark ignited within her. He grabbed hold of her soft thighs and shut his eyes, like he was muttering a prayer or a curse as they rubbed their slick parts together. "Let me help you, darling."

When she couldn't take it anymore, she let him lift her just so, aligning the broad head of his cock with her entrance. She gasped as she sank down, wedging him a little deeper. It was like being split apart. Like he was carving out a part of her she'd held on to for so long. She exhaled slowly, pushing past the bright, delicious pain of his invasion. She was aware of every inch of him filling her, the way his fingers dug into her soft thighs, and the way his breath hitched when she was seated completely against him.

"Fuck," she cursed, surprising herself and Alexander into a short burst of laughter.

"Tell me, darling," he purred. "Tell me what you're feeling."

He'd told her that his body was hers to use, and she intended to touch every part of him. But she wanted him to touch her right back.

"It—it hurts," she said, then hurried to finish when he tensed. "But in a good way. So good. I want you to feel this way, too."

This time, she raised her hips up and slid back down his rigid length in one fell swoop. He sank his head back into the pillows, his face constricted in something like agony as she did it again and again.

"You have no idea how good you feel, darling. How incredible your sweet, tight pussy is." He pumped his hips upward, cupping her ass and guiding her back and forth.

"I want to feel like this forever," she whimpered, seeking out the friction of her clit rubbing against his pelvis. "Like you're deep in my belly. Like no one is ever going to fill me the way you are."

His chest rose and fell quickly, eyes bright and golden and gazing only at her. "Every time you fuck, I want you to think of that. Think of me."

The words were a brand on her skin. He was right, of course. Already she couldn't imagine doing this with anyone else. The idea of it made her chase the sensation, to hold onto it and keep it. Keep him. This beautiful, strong winter god who offered himself as a sacrifice to her pleasure. She only wished he could see himself through her eyes.

THE HEART OF WINTER

Bright tears spilled down her cheeks as her core began to tighten.

"Darling?" Alexander sat up, cradling her against him. Her hard nipples pressed against his pectorals. Long fingers brushed her hair back and cupped her face.

"Don't stop," she begged, tilting her face up to kiss him hard. "Please don't stop."

His palms glided down her spine and rested at her lower back, crushing Lia's body as close as two people could be. And yet, it didn't feel like enough. She rocked up and down his cock, and he soothed the bites he trailed over her shoulder with his tongue until she began to unravel.

"There's a good girl," he rumbled at her ear. "Keep fucking me like that. There's my sweet darling."

My darling. The words lit her up with infinite pleasure. She slammed against him one last time as the feeling became too much. For a moment she tried to run away from it. Too much. Too raw. Too good. But then he gripped the back of her neck and forced her to meet his eyes as he rubbed her harder and she came. The orgasm blooming fast and hard as his dick twitched against the constricting walls of her vagina.

When she was languid and kissing him softly, she eased off him and rolled onto her back, tracing circles around the puckered ridges of her chocolate brown nipples. "Come on me again."

It took him two hard pumps of his fist before ropes of thick, pearlescent semen spilled on her breasts. She had the sudden thought that it reminded her of icing on cupcakes, that she desperately wanted to taste it. But then he distracted her by prying her legs apart and burying his face in her wetness.

She couldn't help the giggles she elicited as he lapped up her orgasm, stroking her tender clit until she felt like she was floating. He teased one finger inside her, then another, curling them like he was calling forth her pleasure.

The candles around them had burned to the wick and were extinguishing one by one. Inhaling the familiar scent of smoke, Lia threaded her fingers through Alexander's thick black hair. When she felt that spark of delicious heat in her belly, she writhed against his face until she was shaking with every wave of her orgasm.

When it was over, she yanked him up to her. She relished the pressure of his strong body against her. How big he was, and yet he still peppered her throat with tender kisses.

He reclined beside her, keeping her close to his chest despite how wet and sticky they both were.

"Well," she said softly.

"Well," he echoed.

Lia wasn't sure what she was supposed to say. Should she thank him? Tell him he was perfect? Ask if she was good? Tell him that she wanted him again, already? Because she did. She loved his tongue and his fingers, but her pussy gave a hard pulse at the thought of his cock. There were too many feelings running through her, and she didn't want to scare him. It helped that they were in the dark. So she settled for being honest.

"Do you know what's weird?" she asked. "I don't feel different."

Alexander teased the short curls on her mound until his index and middle finger found the sensitive heart of her. He rolled slow, lazy circles around it. "How do you feel?"

She bit down on a moan. How was it possible to have gone from not having sex, to constantly needing to have her naked skin touched?

"Like myself. I guess everyone talks about virginity as something you keep so that you can give it away. But to me it was just a part of who I was, and I knew one day I would have sex, but I would still be me. I'm sure it's all the same to you since you've done this a million times. Oh. *Oh*, Alexander." She wriggled against his fingers, her nerves sparking like frayed wires as the rush of her orgasm peaked, surprising and sudden as a storm that had trapped them in the cabin.

He caught her moans with his mouth and kissed her until she felt drunk off him. "I may have been with scores of people, Lia, but I've never been with you until tonight. So no, it's not all the same to me."

Her heart raced at how raw his words were. She didn't know what to say, but he didn't give her a chance either. He tugged her to her feet, and they went into the bath, rinse themselves clean.

When they were finished, she kicked him out of the bathroom. She sat with the realization that she'd had sex. She itched to text her sisters and could practically hear Helena telling her to pee right after. She had a lot of things to think about, but she was too sex drunk and went to crawl into bed.

Alexander was pulling on a robe.

"Where are you going?" she asked, a short whine in her voice.

"I thought you should take the bed."

Something clawed inside of her at the thought of him sleeping anywhere but beside her. She knew she needed to get used to it. They only had a few days together and would soon have to figure a way to get back to reality, back to her world. But she couldn't help it. "Stay. Please. Just for tonight."

He hesitated for a moment. Then she heard the wheeze of the floorboards. The crush of fabric. Felt the pressure of his body on the mattress, then under the covers against her, his arm pinning her to his chest.

"Just for tonight," he whispered.

14
ALEXANDER

Alexander dreamt of a face that had haunted him for years.

Kit ran through the twisting, forbidden paths of the Elfenhörn Forest. They'd been thirteen and spent their days skipping the king's mass and boring lessons. Instead, Alexander sought adventure with his cousin, his brother.

"Wait!" Alexander yelled. Kit had always been the faster runner.

Howls of laughter filled the dark. Animals with glowing red and yellow eyes lit their way through crooked trees. Serpents with iridescent scales shimmered across the damp earth. They'd never been that deep in the ancient forest, and years later, Alexander couldn't recall what they had been searching for. The elusive flower of immortality? To challenge the wicked Elfenhörn king? The thrill of the chase? The chance to see what no one else in the kingdom was allowed to explore?

Whatever it was, they never found it.

The forest had swallowed them whole.

THE HEART OF WINTER

Alexander jerked awake. His heart raced, enveloped by the distinct sensation of falling into the mouth of darkness. He forgot where he was and who he was with. He rubbed at bleary eyes then reached for the burgundy drapery that hung from his four-poster bed to block the sun.

When he grabbed a fistful of air, he blinked at the Guardian's cabin, the clothes scattered across the floor, and the very beautiful woman rousing lazily from sleep. Memories of the previous night flooded him in a fury of heat. The joy and relief at seeing her warred with the jagged edges of his nightmare. It was like Lia's sunshine was too bright and wouldn't let him dwell on the memory of his cousin.

Lia was sprawled on the bed like a lazy kitten. Her dark hair spread against the pillow. Her golden skin still had the faint trace of his magic over her heart and calf, but they were fading. When she rolled on her side, blinking up at him with those midnight eyes and feline smile, a sharp sensation pierced his chest. He rubbed at the spot.

"Hey, you," she said, her voice scratchy with sleep. "Was I snoring?"

Alexander began to laugh, but something above the headboard caught his eye. Something that hadn't been there the day before.

A pale green vine dangled there.

"It can't be," he whispered, climbing out of the bed. Goosebumps peppered every inch of his naked skin, and it had nothing to do with the cold floor, and everything to do with the sprawl of devilbane that had grown overnight. It clung like invasive ivy in an arch over the bed. He pushed the wooden frame aside, Lia gasping as she clung to the mattress.

"What are you doing?" she asked. "What is this stuff?"

"Devilbane," Alexander said gruffly, tearing the vines right where they grew between the cracks of the floorboards and the panels of the wall. The milky green of the plant reminded him of spring in the Eternal Winter Forest. It grew wild in patches, sometimes consuming entire trees.

Lia climbed off the bed and wrapped the bedsheet around her body. "I'm not from your Christmas faerie land, so that means nothing to me. Except it sort of reminds me of mistletoe."

She reached for one of the pale, silver berries that grew in clusters.

He snatched her wrist and gave a warning shake of his head. "Don't touch that."

"Why?" she frowned but did as he asked. "Is it poison?"

"It's used as a sedative. Sometimes to reveal dreams, desires," he said.

"So, it's your world's drug of choice."

Alexander resumed ripping at the overgrown weeds with his fists until he'd gathered most of it. They had come in through the ceiling, the floorboards, a tiny nick in the window where it didn't seal properly.

"This is not supposed to happen. It's supposed to be *over*." He ran downstairs, and Lia followed at his heels. He didn't want to frighten her, but he was doing a terrible job at it. He just knew that he needed to get rid of it, so he threw the bundle of devilbane into the fire. Still green, it would take a moment to get swallowed by the flames, but at least it was done.

"Alex," she said softly. Her long, dark waves were tussled over her bare shoulders. She placed a gentle hand over his biceps, where the Mark of the Saint stopped. "You said it yourself. You got through the solstice, right? Look."

How could her voice cut through to him, pull him back, like he'd reached the end of a very long, dark tunnel and she was a pulse of light guiding his way back? How could her touch focus him into seeing that she was right? The inky marks on his skin hadn't spread.

Of course she was right.

But that didn't explain the devilbane vines sprouting while they slept. He wondered... Perhaps because there was no Saint Nikolas, the magic of the land was wild. Returned to the earth. The cabin *was* partially on the wall that divided the Eternal Winter Forest and Lia's world and that's why it could reach him.

Alexander convinced himself that was the reason for the anomaly. It had to be.

"I'm sorry for scaring you," he told her, standing so still as she ran her fingers down his arms. Everything about her was so soothing. And yet, why was her power over him more terrifying than the pale green vines burning in the fire?

"I'm still trying to understand your world," she said. "When I was little, I used to wonder if legends were real. Mermaids. Vampires. Ghosts. The *Tooth Fairy*."

At that, Alexander's lips curled into a reluctant smile. He rested his palms on her lower back, and settled into the calm that came with her. "Well, I have known of goblins who collect sharp teeth. But they live deep in the northern mountains."

And just like that, everything about that morning was worth it to hear the delighted gasp she made. She clutched her bedsheet to her naked form and nudged him back up the stairs where she plied him with questions about what the goblins looked like (wrinkled and green) and what they used the teeth for (to build their houses, naturally).

After getting dressed, they retired to the kitchen for breakfast. All they had was turkey, but Alexander managed to find a small tray of quail eggs. He cracked the pale brown spotted shells into a pan and watched them pop and blister in the oil.

Lia poured them nettlethorn tea and sighed into her steaming mug. "I miss coffee so much. I mean, I miss my family, too, but coffee is right up there with family."

"What is coffee?" he asked in the same perplexed way she'd asked him what devilbane was.

Her dark eyes brightened as she set her teacup down. That irreverent lock of her hair untucked itself from behind her ear, and he felt the urge to reach and twirl it between his calloused fingers. But she beat him to it.

"Coffee," Lia explained, "is my favorite drink. I suppose since Saint Nikolas left the world in the fourth century, you missed out on this, and several other discoveries."

Alexander felt the sudden urge to show her the kingdom. He'd hated his father and the hypocrisy of the crown, but there were good people there, too. There was beauty in the mountains and rivers. There was the amphitheater and the libraries, the shops with perfumes, and the bakeries offering all kinds of delicacies. Guilt kneaded at his heart. He'd left. He'd been a coward, and he'd left. He couldn't look back. He had no right to.

"Tell me about this coffee drink," he said, clearing his throat.

"Not that your nettlethorn tea isn't great. But there's nothing quite like the smell of freshly ground coffee brewing. My sisters think I'm a monster for drinking it black. Helena loves her vanilla syrup, and Gracie basically puts a splash of coffee in her creamer."

He had no idea what she was saying, but he loved the way her nostrils flared when she got excited. The small crinkles at the edges of her eyes when she smiled that way. He'd die before he allowed her to lose that smile.

The thought pierced through him. What was happening to him? He'd never felt such a thing for anyone except—

A spot of oil landed on his cheek. He cursed but turned to the eggs, nearly overdone. He carefully added an egg on top each of their leftover turkey and set the plates on the table.

"Well, I believe I now have something to add to my list of buckets." He winked at her.

She tugged on her bottom lip. "Finally. I'll make sure I find you the best cup of coffee in town. *If* we ever get to town."

The thought of leaving their cabin bothered him. Was he ready for the world that waited out there? Was he ready to bid Lia, sweet Lia, goodbye?

You have to. She has a family waiting for her, he thought. *She has an entire life that does not include you in it.*

"What about your list?" he asked her. "We *have* crossed off one item."

"Yes, last night was very—uhm—" Her cheeks flushed in the sweetest way, and she looked away from him, but he saw the panic there. "Satisfactory."

"Satisfactory?" Alexander chuckled.

She winced but nodded and shoved a fork full into her mouth. "Mmhm. I mean, I don't want to stroke your ego or anything."

"You are welcome to stroke any part of me, Lia."

"Then, as first times go, I think it'll be memorable."

He'd remember it, too. Just thinking of Lia riding herself to a climax made his cock stir lazily in his trousers. He grinned like the fool he knew he was. Because only a fool would seek out the feelings Lia brought to the surface.

"Well, I should apologize that you waited years for satisfactory." He leaned forward, resting his chin on his threaded fingers, loving the way she fidgeted under his gaze. "If you had another list, perhaps I could help you with it."

"I do," she said, blinking innocently. She produced her magic mirror and tapped it several times until she brought out one of her lists. "Over the years, I've kept a list of things I want to do. Sexually."

He laughed. He couldn't take it anymore. She was too precious. Too perfect.

She narrowed her eyes and turned her cheek to him. "If you're going to laugh, I'll just find someone else to help me with this list when I get home."

The thought of someone else touching her, kissing her, filling her sweet cunt, made him see red. And yet he knew he had no right to her. She wasn't promised to him.

"You misunderstand me, darling," he said. "I was laughing because no one I've ever known has been so detailed with their desires. I was laughing because you are perfect, and everything about you delights me in a way I haven't felt—well—ever, if I'm honest. I'm sorry for making you think I was doing anything but admiring you."

Her eyes were narrowed still, but her pout was unfurling, turning into the wings of a smile. "All right."

"Now, read me this list."

She cleared her throat like she was about to recite an epic poem. He was sure she had a list of her favorite epic poems. "Missionary, which I know is basic, but I just want to try it. Cowgirl, which we did last night, so we're up one. Morning sex, which is more about time than position. Sixty-nine, leapfrog, lotus, wrapped lotus, tabletop, blow job..."

Alexander's abdominal muscles ached from reining in his delight. He didn't want to laugh and cause her to stop reading from her list. But he *was* delighted. "I know not any of these words, sweet Lia. What in the world is a blow job?"

"Well, Helena says you don't actually blow on the penis."

"Ah. I see."

"What do you call it in the Eternal Christmas Land?"

He grumbled lightly. "In the Eternal *Winter Kingdom,* we just ask for a mouth fuck."

"That is *so much* worse!" she shouted, standing up and

taking their empty plates to the sink. "How can you even look at someone and ask for a—I can't even say it."

This time, she laughed first, and he joined her. He couldn't remember the last time he'd laughed so hard it physically hurt.

She scoured the dishes and shook her head indignantly.

"We have several words for sex acts, be sure of that," he said, taking his teacup and standing beside her. For Saint's sake. He couldn't even be a room-width apart from her without being pulled toward Lia.

"Too bad my notebook is back at the B&B, because there are illustrations."

"Oh, I'd love to see your perverted sketches."

She narrowed those dark eyes again. He was starting to like it when she looked at him that way, because his cock gave another nudge.

"They are educational," she said, snatching his teacup mid-sip and washing it. "My family is so tight-lipped about sex. My whole life, the worst thing I could do was be a pregnant teen. Now, the worst thing I could do is not give my parents grandkids even though I'm so not ready and should have thought about that before we had unprotected sex. So, you see, everything I learned about sex was by asking my more experienced friends and sisters."

"And now me." He opened and closed drawers and cupboards.

"What are you looking for?" she asked.

When he opened the cupboard where Elowen kept her dwindling stock of nettlethorn tea, he saw the glass jar of dry red-capped mushrooms. He opened the lid. The scent of freshly turned earth and bitter licorice filled his nose. He took one by the wrinkled stem and held it up to Lia.

"This," he said, "is what we eat in the Eternal Winter Kingdom to prevent pregnancies."

"Can I eat it if I'm not from your world?" She leaned forward and sniffed it, like he was offering her a rose. He did rather wish he had something prettier to give her.

"Only one of us needs to take it for it to work," he said, popping it into his mouth. "The effects last several days, but I don't like to take my chances."

"What does it taste like?"

"Like a bitter, dry mushroom." He washed it down with a new bottle of cider he opened. "Actually, there is something I must tell you, so it doesn't surprise you."

"Just so we're clear," she said, refilling her teacup with nettlethorn brew. "Nothing good ever starts with that kind of statement. I'm already imagining the literal worst things."

He took a deep breath and set his cider down. He paced to the wooden beam that split the kitchen and leaned against it, always facing her. "As you know, I was my father's spare, but even though my brothers carried most of the powers of Nikolas, I had dregs of it. For me, it manifested into pleasure."

She nearly choked on her tea. "Your superpower is sex? Is that what you're trying to tell me?"

"I'm trying to tell you that every part of me is meant to give pleasure to those I take to bed. I've had women claim I cured their melancholy. After I fucked a pianist, he went to write the most celebrated sonata in the kingdom. My very seed takes on the taste of my lover's appetite."

It was Lia's turn to laugh. "I'm already going out on a limb by believing that you're from some place called the Eternal Winter Kingdom and that you are the great-times-a-thousand-grandson of *thee* Saint Nikolas. But I watched you come out of that portal, and I saw the mark grow on your skin, and I saw you heal me. However, this—magical tasting sperm isn't biologically possible."

"I seem to be the only person the magic doesn't work on, as

THE HEART OF WINTER

the cruel hands of fate have determined."

She grinned wickedly, hitching one eyebrow as a question. "You've tried it?"

Then he was thinking of it. Of spilling into Lia's pretty, plump mouth and kissing her as she positively dripped with him. Fuck. He felt his erection strain against trousers that were already too tight on him. He could barely form words, and so he nodded.

Lia's eyelids fluttered slowly. Was she imagining what he was?

She tapped her nails on the faded roses painted on the sides of the porcelain. He'd never wanted to read someone's mind the way he did with her. It was like she was deciding, making a list in her mind.

The cabin was the kind of quiet which made background noises loud. The crack of the fire in the other room. The small creaks from the wooden slats in the ceiling. The frenzied rhythm of his heart. The clip of porcelain as Lia set her teacup on the counter. The whisper of her bare feet as she padded toward him.

"I want to try it," she whispered, resting her palms over his heart.

"I already told you, Lia. My body is yours." He leaned forward, brushing the tip of his nose with the round bud of hers. She raised her lips for a kiss. It had only been hours, but he'd wanted to kiss her all morning before he'd ruined it with his tantrum and the cursed devilbane.

She ran her hands down his torso, whimpering when she went lower still to find him already hard. She undid the buttons and pulled his erection free.

He gasped as she gripped his base to hold him tight as she lowered herself to her knees. She gaped at his cock with wide eyes.

"I almost forgot how big you were," she said, peering up at him. Squeezing and letting go. Tracing the pale green veins sprouting across his tender flesh. It was like she was testing his limits. Testing how her touch affected him.

He rocked his head back and hit the wooden beam. The slight pain helped him focus, because he already wanted to break apart, just from her slight touch and her breathy sighs and her sweet, sweet awe-filled voice.

She kissed up his length then licked under his frenulum. With a sweep of her tongue, she circled the pink head of his cock, flicking at the opening there where his seed beaded in clear droplets.

"I don't taste anything yet," she said, a small laugh hitched there.

"You have to get to the end, darling," he said roughly.

He panted as she took his head into her plush mouth and let her tongue encircle him slowly, releasing him with a pop that made him curse. Lia's big innocent eyes locked on his as she took his head deeper, her long lashes blinking fast when he felt the resistance of her throat. She whimpered and gagged.

He brushed her hair back, caressed the side of her face. "We can stop."

His cock was slick with her saliva, and she used it to give him long, delicious jerks. Her beautiful features were set in stubborn resolve. "No, I can take it."

And she did, this time, ready for the abrasion of his head against the back of her throat. He felt every sigh, every whimper, every murmur of delight vibrating through him.

Fuck. *Fuck.* He'd been touched a hundred, a thousand times before. He'd fucked and kissed his way through the kingdom. But he had never been touched like this. He had never been touched by her. She was going to break him. She would be the thing that tipped him over. And when it was finished and she left him for the safety of her normal world, he'd thank her and vanish into the cold exile he'd wanted from the start. But first, he had to give her the bliss she desired. After all, that was the power he'd transfigured his body into.

She braced her hands at his thighs, digging half-moon impressions into his flesh.

"My wicked little darkling." His breath hitched as she let the top of her teeth graze the velvet skin of his head then licked at the spot with her expert tongue. He pulled on her hair, his blood rushing through him like liquid flame. "I'm going to come. I'm going to fucking come."

She dug her nails in deeper at his thighs. Her eyes were bright and expectant, and he wanted to be anything, be everything she wished for.

"Lia," he groaned as a wave of pleasure snapped low in his belly. His cock seized, and he watched surprise flood her features, pearl-white seed trickling down the corners of her mouth as she eased back. He gave a rough exhale as she swallowed, the muscles of her throat the most perfect thing he'd ever seen. She licked the delicate bow of her upper lip, her large eyes on his.

"You taste—"

She got to her feet and leaned in close. He kissed her. She tasted of him, bitter and salty, and she'd been such a good girl taking in his huge cock, like she'd done it time and time again.

He pulled back and asked, "What does your pleasure taste like?"

She burrowed into his side. Her nipples were hard through her sweater, and he felt every inch of her. In the golden candlelight, he hadn't realized that there were tears at the corners of her eyes, and he kissed them reverently.

"Honey, Alexander," she whispered, and kissed him deeply. "Milk and honey."

15

LIA

Lia loved fairytales. When she was a little girl, her grandmother used to tell her stories of young girls getting snatched by shadowy elfish men in provincial towns of South America. When her grandmother had passed, she'd left the love of stories behind. Wonder and magic under hills and faraway places.

As she lazed on the fur throws in front of the fireplace, Lia let it sink in, *really sink in*, that perhaps she was one of those fairytale humans she'd spent her whole life reading about.

After all, she was snowed in with a winter god. A runaway prince. A king who had abdicated his crown for reasons she couldn't truly understand. In her eyes, he was more than worthy. In her eyes, he was brave and strong and adoring. Sweet, quite literally.

A restless shiver ran through her at what they had done that morning. He'd tasted like paradise, like the rivers of Eden, milk and honey...and her favorite ice cream. It was impossible, but she'd also seen miracles that shattered her sense of reality. She considered pinching herself awake, but her inner thighs already ached. It was the kind of ache that made her floaty and languid.

Fire-kissed as she lounged on the settee in front of the roaring logs.

She woke up, not having realized she'd dozed off. When checked her phone she saw it was well past lunch. The battery life was halfway depleted. Anxiety frayed at her heart because it was the longest time she'd spent without her sisters. She hoped that her last message had gone through as an SMS, but there was no way to tell. With the snow piled up outside, they weren't going anywhere.

For now, Lia was content being a princess in the woods snowed in with a winter god who was helping her fulfill her sex fantasies.

As if she'd summoned him with her pervy little thoughts, Alexander sauntered down the creaky wooden stairs. His raven hair was damp, a stubborn wave, flopped onto his brow. The sweater he'd pulled on was completely ripped at the seams where sleeves must have been, showcasing the sculpted muscles of his forearms and biceps.

She propped herself up on her side and caught the moment where he touched the edge of his Saint's Mark, like he was making sure it hadn't moved. Like it was too good to be true that he had escaped that destiny.

Lia knew exactly what "too good to be true" felt like because it was her reaction that very morning when she'd woken up he was the first thing she saw. When he'd made breakfast. When he'd come in her mouth. Now, when he sat down right beside her and let his eyes linger on her lips.

He adjusted the front of his trousers, trying for discreet, but she had already noticed the bulge there. The sight of it made her heart skip. She did that to him. By just lying there in front of the fire.

"What are you smiling about?" he asked, resting his hand on her hip.

Was it normal for such a small, casual touch to make her skin feel so tight again? She tried to remember everything her sisters had taught her about the after-effects of sex, but the words just turned into a bunch of little thought clouds and evaporated. They couldn't help her, and besides, Lia was starting to realize that no one in the entire world might understand what she was feeling and going through. She had to figure it out on her own.

"You," she answered. "What did those sleeves ever do to you?"

He chuckled lightly and extended one of his arms out. "I'll have to figure out a way to replenish the Guardian's wardrobe."

"Do you think she's stuck over there?" Lia asked. "Shouldn't she have returned?"

His grip on her tightened as worry crisscrossed lines on his forehead. "I do not know. Last I saw her was at the great banquet. The— The only body I saw was the king's." Alexander blinked his worry at the fireplace. "But Hans will have sorted everything out."

Lia wanted to say that it was a lot to hope for, but she knew he needed to believe that. Otherwise, he'd be consumed by guilt. Lia wanted to comfort him, but when he turned to her, his face clear of worry.

"Do you want tea, darling?" he asked.

"I think I'd like something stronger."

Alexander returned with a tray carrying two healthy pours of whisky and the bottle they were nearly finished drinking. Beside it was a tin of stale cookies and cold turkey. She would have given her first born for a cheeseburger and fries. They ate first, and she took the opportunity to ask him more about his home. The village, the people. She wondered how a place could exist, hidden in the ether. The impossibility of magic was almost overwhelming. He'd run away from it, but there she was, wanting more of it.

At least she had him.

As the day grew long, she lay on her belly, angled toward Alexander and the fire. The whisky burned down her throat. "Alexander..."

"Noelia..."

"You obviously know about my first time, but I was curious about yours."

He cocked an eyebrow, seemingly more amused than bothered at her curiosity. "Well, the story I've always told is that on the night of the summer hawthorn moon, the Hellebörne coven marks the half of the year by feeding the land with bacchanals fueled by their carnal energies."

"Like orgies and stuff?"

"Precisely like orgies and stuff," he said. "It's desperate, making sure that the Eternal Winter Forest remains a paradise. When I was younger, I always searched the wood for their location, but it was private. If the coven wanted you there, you'd find your way. If they didn't, you spent the night with blue balls in the woods. And then finally, one lucky night, the meadow revealed itself to me, and I was among the fray."

"And that was your first time?"

"No," he said, his throat rippling as he swallowed his drink. "That is how the story ends. Earlier that month a very pretty apprentice at my uncle's Alchemy workshop had arrived from the countryside. She specialized in crossbreeding seeds that could grow in any climate, and I loved her. Or I thought I did. I was sixteen, therefore I loved any pretty thing that would look in my direction. But her— For a month she found her way to my side. She left me flowers she bred herself. Flashed smiles at me during banquets. Whispered promises in my ear. Told me she'd die without me. At the end of the month, I worked up the courage. I kissed her. She led me back to her suite. The place reeked of peonies." He scrunched up his nose, like even the ghost of the scent bothered him.

"It was clumsy and awkward, and I came before I could properly get undressed. In my own foolish way, I thought it was perfect. I didn't know any better."

He met Lia's gaze, and there was a moment where he hesitated. It wasn't the first time she though that he was holding back.

"Go on," she prompted.

"Later that night, I filched a string of pearls from the vault and presented her with a promise of marriage. I was a fool. So young. Desperate for—" He caught himself and shook his head. "She told me that it had all been a mistake. That I was a mistake. That her heart belonged to someone more worthy."

"That's horrible. Who the fuck?" Lia was afraid to touch him, so she only listened.

"My brother, Hansel." Alexander drained his teacup.

"Alex—" she said. "Alexander."

He brushed a thumb over her bottom lip. "I like when you call me Alex. Only Kit used to call me that."

"I'm so sorry." She wanted to rewind time to never ask the question in the first place. "I sort of thought it would have been something less cruel."

"That's all right, sunshine," he said and found that he meant it. "I hadn't been in love with her, not truly. I think if I had, I would have found a way to forgive her, to make her mine. Instead, that night, I found the Hellebörne bacchanal and fucked my way into a serious edification of the human body."

Lia sucked in a sharp breath. He couldn't be sure if she was turned on or horrified. Perhaps both. "But your brother—"

"I suppose I'm laughing in the end. Once Hansel tired of her, she returned to the countryside, heartbroken. Alas, it is not the story you expected. But I gave you one of my stories. Now I want to know something."

She sat up, refilling their teacups, her core humming with anticipation. "Okay..."

"Why did you choose a wretched fuck like me?"

"You're not wretched." His amber eyes glanced away as she said the words. She propped herself up on her knees and cupped his face in her hands, forcing their eyes to meet. "You're not wretched. You're the most beautiful man I've ever seen in any realm."

Alexander pressed his forehead to hers. "You are too good, Lia."

"Well, if we're being honest...Part of me thinks that maybe I wasn't being picky. All those other times? It was like I wanted something to go wrong because it never felt right. Almost like I was just waiting for you. You've shown me the man you are. Brave, strong, sweet, a little broken. And I—"

Lia stopped herself from saying words she wouldn't be able to take back. She brushed her lips to his with a feather-light touch. "I know what I want from whoever comes next."

Alexander went rigid at her words. The movement was so jarring, she pulled back to make sure he hadn't turned to literal stone. His face clouded with darkness and anger. Was it something she'd said? Had he intuited that she was about to confess how much she cared about him? Was he freaked out about her confession?

"I'll get dinner started," she said.

"Lia—"

"No, don't worry. It's my turn."

She tossed another couple of logs in the fireplace, pleased with how well the city-girl she was had adapted to the magical cabin. In the kitchen, as she assembled the left-over turkey and set some sad potatoes to boil, she cursed at herself for revealing too much. She wanted to blame it on the fireplace, the furs, the soft lighting and glow, his piercing eyes.

Finally, she remembered some of the things Helena and Gracie had warned her about. Catching feelings. What did she really expect was going to happen? He'd fall in love with her, and they would stay in the cabin forever? He was from a mythical land, and she was fairly certain the Eternal Winter Forest wasn't covered by the Schengen states.

When it was time for dinner, he quietly set the table. They ate the potatoes she'd boiled then pan-fried to crisp up the skin. They devoured the rest of the turkey, and Lia was positive she might never have the bird ever again. He plied her with questions about her father's restaurant, her sisters, and it was a volley of reminders that there was a world waiting for her, a world he perhaps didn't fit into. For that very reason, she needed to stop the emotions attempting to mutiny in her brain.

But when they returned to the living room and he curled up on the couch, picking up an old hardcover to read to her, Lia knew she was done for. His voice was melodic, hypnotizing as he turned page after page, reciting fables he'd read as a kid. Men with fox faces who waited for human villagers to make deals with in the moonlight. Saint Nikolas the First defeating the beast under the hill in the Elfenhörn Forest. Frost giants, permanently asleep in the mountains to the north.

"It sounds magical," she said softly.

Alexander nodded but said nothing else to agree. "Lia— Earlier today—"

"You don't have to say anything."

He closed the book and set it on the coffee table cluttered with their dwindling bottle of whisky and delicate porcelain teacups. "But I do."

"No, you don't." She flattened the backs of her hands on her eyes, like she could squash the embarrassment that was bubbling to the surface. "I said too much, and that's why you got all disgruntled and weird."

Alexander smiled. Actually smiled at her ridiculousness. He took her hands in his. She felt that tightness again, just from his touch.

"My reaction had nothing to do with the things you said about me. No one has ever held me in the same regard. I don't deserve it." He swallowed hard but didn't look away when he continued. "It's what you said after. Whoever comes next. The very thought of someone else touching you, kissing you, fucking you. It lit up a rage I have never felt."

"Oh," she said in an exhale.

"You owe me nothing, darling." Alexander pressed a kiss to her knuckles. "We have not exchanged vows. I made you a promise, but I have no right to claim you. To make you mine and only mine. Please, forgive me."

There was nothing to forgive. Hearing him say that he wanted to make her his, and only his, had her crawling across the settee and onto his lap. Grabbing hold of his very muscular thighs, she leaned forward and kissed his cheeks, his temples, his parted lips. He kissed her back hard, taking hold of her and tumbling her to the sprawl of furs on the floor, her arms pinned over her head.

She offered up her throat for him to lick and suck the sensitive place he had discovered there. The hard landscape of his body crushing the softness of her breasts. She parted her legs to better feel the hard ridge of his cock stimulate her clothed pussy.

When Lia tried to reach down to undo his trousers, she felt resistance. At first, she smiled against his kisses. He was holding her wrists so roughly, not at all like the night before. But then she felt his hands at her waistband tugging at the drawstring to wiggle the fabric over her thighs. How was he doing both? Had she lost time? When had he tied her up?

As she struggled, the bindings at her wrists tugged back and the moan she let out surprised her.

She angled back to see that it wasn't Alexander or ropes. It was a spool of pale green vines.

The devilbane was back.

16

ALEXANDER

This is impossible, Alexander's mind thundered. Curling milky green vines had slid between the floorboards and wound their way around Lia's wrists. She pulled and pulled, but it only seemed to make them get tighter.

"What the fuck?" Lia cried out. Every time she wriggled, she brought her damp heat snugly against his cock.

Alexander sat up, keeping her lower body steady with his weight. He snatched the devilbane vines and ripped them apart. Then gathered Lia into his lap and examined her wrists. Her skin was pink where the bloody vines had hurt her. He pressed reverent kisses there, and wished he had that wretched curse only to heal her.

"I'm all right," she said, glancing at the way the vines still moved, undulating like serpents.

"This isn't supposed to be happening," he said darkly and reached for the place where the Mark of the Saint marred his flesh. He searched the room for a weapon. Something to uproot the devilbane. He'd never heard of *sentient* devilbane, but he'd put an end to it.

Lia worried her bottom lip, swollen from his devouring kisses. "*Wait.*"

"What do you mean, wait?"

She stayed him with a hand to his chest where she felt his heart beat with fear. "I think they're reacting to you."

"I—I've never heard of such a thing."

"You said it yourself. There has always been a Nikolas. Maybe you're still connected to the kingdom?"

He shook his head. "I can't be. The Mark isn't finished."

"Think about it," she said. "This morning they appeared after we slept together. Now they're back. What were you thinking of?"

Flame rushed to every part of him. His cock was so hard, so very hard, and he needed release. "I was thinking that I wanted to feel the pulse thrum on your pretty little neck while I fucked you. That I wanted to pin you down and devour you until your body remembers me and only me."

"I—" She was breathing fast, and he imagined how the inner walls of her secret place must be fluttering like her long lashes. "I want that, too."

"Lia," he growled her name. Part of him wanted to see if her intuition was right. If the devilbane was reacting, somehow, to his desire for her. Part of him thought about being a coward and running again, where no magic could find him. But all of him wanted her. All of him *needed* her. He had always been reckless with his body, yes, but never with his heart. Slowly, he was becoming undone by her, and he was letting it happen. "You've done this to me."

"Because you want me?" she whispered. Her large, innocent eyes swallowed him up with their darkness. He tipped her back on the floor until she was burrowing on the furs. She drew her arms over her head, a wicked smile playing on her lips as she dared him to summon the self-control to stay away from her.

"Yes," he said, and even the single word was a ragged sound as he ripped her sweater down the center and exposed her breasts. He took the brown circle of her nipple into his mouth and worked his way down to strip her trousers off. "I want you naked and wet and there for my pleasure. I want to find you sprawled on these furs with your legs open for me, waiting for me. Every time you come, you say only my name."

The vines grew and gathered, winding around her wrists, holding her like an altar offering on a full moon. He stripped off his clothes, and she shut her eyes and sighed so prettily that he had to blink and make sure she was real. Her hair was a tangle of dark waves, her naked body like an hourglass of decadence. He cinched her narrow waist with his hands to elicit a gasp.

"If it's too much, you must tell me, Lia," he said.

She pulled on the vines holding her. "What if I want it to be too much?"

"Fuck, Lia, you're going to destroy me." He slid back down, kissing a trail that ended with his tongue stroking open the cleft of her pussy. He needed to taste her and stroke her. To know she was ready for him. She cried out, squeezing him with her thighs.

"Please, Alex," she said. "Please."

It was the *please* that undid him. He covered her body with his, nudging her knees open. She raised her hips to chase his length, but he denied her. He slid against her slit, wetting himself until she begged, and the vines split like the head of a hydra. A thin thread of the palest green wound itself around her throat.

Then, Alexander thrust inside her, kissing away the little moans she made. She was wrapped up, just for his pleasure, and he still wanted more. He wanted to fuse with her the way the sun and moon did during an eclipse. He wanted to be the stars on the expanse of skin.

"Oh God, Alex. I want you so much," she panted, and he felt the start of her orgasm twitching around his shaft. "Deeper. Deeper, please."

If he were any deeper, he'd be in her throat, he thought. But he cupped her generous rump and tilted her hips up. She was so slick and wet, and his cock glided inside, hard and fast and desperate. So desperate, the devilbane was everywhere now, tying their bodies together and winding around his own throat, and it had never felt this good before, this rooted to something or someone else before. The thought shot fear up his spine, but it was chased away quickly by the contractions of her pussy around his cock.

"I'm coming," Lia said, bright with surprise. Every rut and thrust made her cry out in delighted whimpers.

He rested his palm around her throat, feeling the erratic pulse under the trickles of vines, the shimmer of crushed berries on her skin, and waited until the final waves of her pleasure left her languid.

She raised her lips for a kiss he met with fervor. He ripped apart the vines holding them together and pulled out of her.

Lia got eagerly to her knees and pressed her lips to the glistening head of his cock. He groaned and stroked his way into release.

"You're bloody perfect," he said as she lapped him up like a sated kitten.

When they were finished, Alexander tossed the torn vines into the fire. The devilbane had stopped moving when he'd admitted how much he'd wanted Lia. It bothered him that he couldn't understand why this was happening. He'd explore in the morning, perhaps. For now, he had a beautiful, insatiable darling to tend to.

His insatiable darling.

❧ 17 ❦
LIA

Lia never expected to have "sentient vines tie me up and choke me when I get fucked" on her list of sex fantasies, but she was through the looking glass. In the morning she woke up with that delicious soreness in her muscles. Alexander still slumbered, so she pressed a quick kiss on his temple and crept to use the bathroom and wash up.

Downstairs, dressed in a loose tunic and green wool leggings, Lia threw another log on the fire. They were burning through the wood quickly, and even though Alexander had cut down a literal tree, the logs were severely depleted, as was their food.

She went to the kitchen and lit several taper candles. She was tempted to find a hammer and remove the nails bolting the shutters closed, but part of her worried that they'd have another mini storm blast. Alexander's power was supposed to be gone, but after last night, she was sure they were missing something. Whatever it was, they'd deal with it together.

The memory of the previous night, of how deeply he'd wanted her, sent waves of shivers up her arms. She never thought she'd be into someone feeling jealous, but Alexander being jealous of a hypothetical man who would come after... Lia couldn't even imagine the thought.

This can't last, she reminded herself as she rummaged through the meager contents of the pantry. She swallowed the stone of uneasiness that came with their inevitable end.

She found a jar of dark cherries in syrup. Though, since they were in a magical cabin, it could have been tiny fermented livers or hearts. Nothing could surprise her. At least, she hoped.

By the end of her search, Lia lined up all their food on the counter. Two more quail eggs. A skinny bulb of garlic. A cloth bag of walnuts. Four golden beets and a bundle of dry rosemary. Not to mention the second turkey in the ice box. Her stomach rumbled, so she fried the eggs, cracked a bunch of the walnuts, and put them in a bowl.

That's how Alexander found her when he made his way to the kitchen. His eyes were still narrow with sleep, his hair mussed up and adorable. She imagined him as a little boy, waking up the same way, and a chasm opened in her chest because she'd heard glimpses of his childhood. Lonely, scared, cruel. It made the smile he flashed her feel like a gift.

He made nettlethorn tea and ate one of those licorice dirt mushrooms. They ate in the kind of easy silence she loved, though she still hungry immediately after finishing their breakfast.

As if he could read her thoughts, he reached out and brushed her hair back. "We're low on stores. We have two options. You can stay here, safe and sound, and I can—"

"You lost me," she said and let go of an exasperated sigh. "It's never good when two people split up from the abandoned cabin. I know you don't have movies where you're from, but in my world, it's always bad news bears."

He sipped his tea, brows shooting up in confusion. "You have bears delivering your news?"

She snorted and kissed him. So big and handsome and yet so *literal*. "We're not splitting up. I can bundle up. Besides. The storm has stopped. We just have to wade through snow and make sure we don't fall into a lake and get lost."

"Right," he said. "*Just* that."

"It's been sunny. The snow must have melted a bit." She ate another walnut, the buttery taste earthy and rich. "Besides, we don't have to go right now. We have food enough for today and tomorrow." She gasped. "Tomorrow is Christmas Eve."

"Ah," he said in that unreadable way of his.

"I love Christmas Eve. I just realized I've never missed it."

Alexander leaned forward, and she felt herself warm under his amber gaze. "What do you love about it?"

"My parents cook all day. My sisters and I decorate for the big party. We have way too much spiked cider from our neighbors." She sighed at the memory. "Then we dance and tell the same stories we do every year and dance again. At midnight we open presents."

"It sounds like the winter solstice."

"Well, your ancestor is the inspiration for my Santa Claus." Lia smirked, enjoying the little growl he made. "And he comes down the chimney, bringing presents for all the good kids."

"That again." Alexander poured himself more tea. "Yes, yes, we've had humans from your realm bring the stories to the Eternal Winter Kingdom."

"You have?" she asked. "How does that work?"

"Some royals have sent knights into this realm to see the development of the world and bring back things that may be of use. Sometimes we honor artists, musicians, playwrights, inventors."

Lia thought of the faerie stories about humans getting kidnapped or stumbling into the fairyland. There's truth to the myths, then. "Do the humans ever make it back?"

"Naturally," Alexander said. "Though some choose to stay."

Would she have chosen to stay if she had found herself there? Or would she have run for the safety of home because all she did was dream up lists of things she *might* do but never actually put anything into motion? The thought, brutally honest, was one she didn't usually let herself linger on. There was no reason to. And besides, it didn't matter because soon she'd be back home.

"Well, it's still my favorite holiday," she said.

"Tell me a favorite memory, then."

She pondered it for a long moment, tangling her fingers with his, warm from holding the teacup. "I think every year it's a little different. I'm not even sure if I remember different parts and mix them into one big Christmas collage or what. But I guess...there was one year. The last one that I believed in Santa Claus."

He barked a laugh. "You believed?"

"No laughing," she warned.

"Carry on."

"You've seen Santa Claus, right?"

"As perverse as it is, yes. Not to mention the little *toy* you carried with you."

She ignored him and continued. "My sisters were all asleep. I was seven, and even though I'm the middle sister, I think I'm the most gullible. Or maybe I've always wanted to believe in something. Anyway, I went downstairs and left the milk and cookies."

Alexander looked up to the ceiling, like he was asking the ancients for patience. "A fortifying snack for the Saint of Wonders. Do go on."

"I get down there and I find Saint Nicholas himself." She ignored the wounded grumble he released. "All dressed in red velour and a white beard and white hair. And he was making out with my mother!"

"The scandal," he said in mock disbelief. "Even in my world, no one wants to be a cuckold."

"Not a cuckold. It was my dad. I'd been so mad at him for working all day and missing the party. That was when the restaurant first opened, and he was always at work. But even though he was tired, he still dressed up and put presents under our tree. Though in hindsight, I wonder if my mom also had a Santa Claus fantasy."

"Also?" he asked, squeezing her hand, humor saturating his voice. "Does that mean my ancestor is your fantasy?"

"You're my fantasy," she said, her heart racing as she spoke the words.

Alexander grinned, but his voice was lower, rougher. "What happened then?"

"I went back to sleep. I knew in that moment that Santa Claus wasn't real, but my father was. My father, who sacrificed and worked hard. I think I internalized it. I threw myself into school and work. I wanted him to be proud of me, but it turned into my parents depending on me too much. Now he wants me to inherit a failing restaurant. He even gave George his blessing even though I told my mother I wasn't happy."

At the mention of George, she watched the ripple of agitation along the muscles of his jaw. "If you'd stayed, would you have settled for a lesser love simply to appease your family?"

Lia met Alexander's eyes, clear as honey in the candlelight. "There was a moment when I thought it would be so easy. Even if I wasn't *happy* happy. Even if I wasn't madly in love. I'd be fine. But now—"

"Now?" he whispered.

She shrugged. "Near-death experiences will make you realize there's more to life than duty. But you know all about that. I think I made the right choice calling it off."

They sat there, staring at each other, for a while longer. Alexander's hand traced lazy circles on her thigh. She drained her teacup. She'd never felt so at ease. At peace.

"What about you?" Lia asked. "Didn't you ever catch your parents? Though I suppose it wouldn't be a fetish where you're from..."

"I—I never knew my mother actually." As he spoke the words, he held her hand a little tighter.

She winced. He'd mentioned that his mother had fallen ill after his birth. *Dammit, Lia.* "I'm so sorry. I wasn't thinking."

"Darling, it's all right." But he shut his eyes for a moment too long. His dark lashes fluttered before looking at her again. "I do not know how to miss someone I never knew."

She hated the deep hurt in his voice. He tried to clear his throat, and drank more tea, but she saw it there in the flecks of gold among the amber.

"I have composites of her," he said after a moment, "like your memories of your Christmas Eve. Stories from a cobbler, a baker, a farmer. All the people who had been touched by her grace and kindness only ever said how perfect she was. How beautiful. Golden like the twilight during the winter solstice. I knew that she loved horseback riding. She loved her garden. Attending the opera. She loved reading in the village library even though the royal library was bigger. I have a hundred stories, perhaps more from strangers. But none from my own father or brothers. Like he kept her memory from me because he blamed me. He blamed me because I lived, and she died, and it was such a waste."

When he shut his eyes, a single luminous tear ran down his

cheek. She leaned forward and caught it with her lips. She wanted to absorb his sadness. To get rid of the twisted feelings that made him doubt himself.

"How could your own father say that to you?"

Alexander did not answer. She saw the war of emotions on his features, felt it in the way he held her like she was a life raft and he was adrift on a cold sea.

When the tea got cold, and her fingers began to cramp, she brushed a kiss to his lips. He blinked around the room, at her, and smiled.

"I have decided that you and I are going to celebrate Christmas Eve. Tonight."

Lia smiled so widely it hurt. "Tonight?"

"There are solstice decorations for the tree, and we have that turkey." He tugged her onto his lap, and she ground her ass against his swelling cock. "There should be a dress somewhere in Elowen's closet. I can't promise music, but I do know a few other activities we can do."

"It sounds perfect," she said, kissing him slow and long until the feeling built at the pit of her stomach and she was tugging down her leggings. She sat back on his hard length. His cock so snug with her knees pressed together. He banded an arm around her waist and yanked her hair back to kiss her bare throat as she rocked and rubbed herself into an orgasm, and he pulled out of her, sliding his cock between her ass cheeks, and came in warm rivulets. It ran down her lower back and on his abdomen.

She adjusted herself on his lap, dragging a finger along his stomach. She brought the glistening semen to her lips. He uttered a jagged curse and kissed her. It was the kind of kiss that soothed something inside of her she hadn't known had withered. She both wanted more sex and to curl into his arms and go back to sleep, but Alexander had other plans and was already cleaning her up.

"Come, now, sunshine." He took her hand like he was leading her into the great hall of a palace and she was his princess. "We have a feast to prepare."

18

ALEXANDER

What had Alexander been thinking? *Christmas Eve?* He'd spent years hating the celebrations at the palace. And yet, he was hunched over in the tiny underground cellar, accumulating wooden splinters from the crate of decorations. Luckily, he found a bottle of whisky covered in dust and brought that upstairs, too. He felt utterly ridiculous. He'd left his kingdom so he wouldn't have to think about his legacy, the winter solstice, and everything that he'd abandoned. But there he was, losing control over himself like he was under some sort of enchantment.

It wasn't magic, though.

It was the power of Lia. The way she made him want to cut himself open and reveal the hideous parts of his soul, the things he never voiced to anyone. The useless runt, spare, scoundrel, rake. The unworthy son.

He knew that once they left the cabin, their lives would diverge. But in the meantime, he was going to give her the celebration that made her miss home because Lia deserved the world. He had nothing to offer her but his wretched heart and his giant cock. And yes, this, this small celebration...this he could do.

When he tumbled out of the cellar, hitting his head on the low ceiling hatch built for the squat Guardians of old, Lia clapped for him like he was her triumphant hero. Every splinter and the dust making his eyes water was worth it.

They decorated the tree Elowen had left bare. He tried to focus on Lia's bright eyes and full smiling lips, the way she hummed songs he didn't know the lyrics to. But worry for the Guardian wedged under his skin. She hadn't returned. She hadn't returned because something worse must have happened, and he'd left, and he hadn't taken the Nikolas mantle, and why in the world had he thought Hansel would do the right thing? A pool of bitter dread gathered in the pit of his stomach.

"Are these silver nipple clamps?" Lia asked, her voice cutting through his dark thoughts. He homed in on the curious pinch of her nose, realizing what she was holding.

"Ah, those are candle holders."

"Really? That feels like a fire hazard."

"It's perfectly safe." He clipped one to a center branch, then wedged a thin candle in the circle slot. "As long as the tree is fresh and watered."

She set her hands on her hips. "Tell me one of these Christmas trees has never burned down in your palace?"

"A *Yule* tree has never burned down in the palace. Except..." He narrowed his eyes as if he could see the memory blooming in his mind. "That one year when I set the tree in the great hall on fire on purpose."

"Why?"

"I think the question you should be asking is 'why ever not?'"

"If we'd known each other as children, I would have been the annoying girl who kept a running list of every bad thing you ever did and then snitched on you. I snitched on my sisters all the time."

He reached into the crate and unpacked the wooden reindeer carvings. He thought of Kilian and hoped his friend had returned to his forest. "And I would have shoved you into the nearest bog."

"Hey!"

"I'd save you and then earn a kiss."

She rolled her eyes. "As if. Though you'd deserve a bog kiss for being so mean."

He blew dust from a box of multicolored blown glass orbs. When they caught the firelight, they reflected prisms of color. As they hung them, he remembered the day he ate her cunt and his magic unraveled into the hundreds of lights. His cock twitched, then he sobered as he grazed the unfinished mark on his arm.

It's over, he assured himself, but then doubt wedge under his skin. *What if it isn't?*

"So, tomorrow," Lia said. Alexander didn't miss the nervous hitch in her voice. "I've been thinking we should try to find the village market where I got lost. Do you know where you'll go?"

Alexander clipped another candle. Strung another bauble. His fingers were sticky with the scent of pine. "I haven't been able to think about it. You have a very demanding schedule."

"Because fulfilling my virginal sex fantasies is such a chore." She winked, and with just the bat of those lashes, the pout of her eager mouth. He was hard again. "Seriously though. Do you have a plan?"

He did not. His only intention had been to run like a coward because he hadn't wanted to take up a legacy he'd scorned. Who had he left to suffer? He hadn't thought of anyone but himself because he was selfish and worthless.

"I will do what the first Nikolas did," Alexander said. "I will find a secluded place in a far, quiet corner of the world and live out the rest of my days alone."

Lia raised her eyebrows. She shook the branches, adjusted the silver candle clips. "He didn't live alone, though. He had followers and became a king."

Alexander hadn't considered that. Of course, the legend spoke of his ancestor's intention. His miraculous defeat of the evil in the forest and his ascension to a throne he never set out to claim.

"Then," Alexander said, "I suppose I'll do what Saint Nikolas couldn't." Even as he said it, the words felt hollow.

"You don't have to, you know." She didn't look at him. Wouldn't look at him. "My sister's a lawyer. She could probably find the right person to get you a birth certificate and papers. You could have a real life."

"I don't deserve a real life." His words felt weak, like a whisper. He wasn't sure if she'd even heard him at first. Then she stepped around the tree to sidle up beside him. The sight of her, patient and *adoring*—it hurt parts of him he didn't even know were bruised.

She rested her palms over his heart. "I can't convince you of what you deserve. You won't believe me when I tell you that you are worthy. You're worthy to me. You made the choice to leave your kingdom, and you can make the choice to be something else. Something that your brothers and father can't touch because they're not here with you. I am. And—I'm not ready to say goodbye to you."

"I'm not ready to say goodbye to you either," he said, taking her chin and tilting her face to his. There were still too many jagged pieces in his heart for that to happen. But perhaps, perhaps he could imagine a path he'd never anticipated he'd take. "Then let tonight not be a celebration of farewells, but of new beginnings."

She kissed him, slow and reverent. He inhaled the scent of pine and woodsmoke. The fragrant oils on her skin, and the aroma beneath that which he could only recognize as Lia. His Lia.

When the tree was finished, the last ornament her wooden Santa Claus trinket, they put the turkey in the oven and then dressed for dinner.

She'd been up there for so long, his nerves twisted in the pit of his stomach. Why couldn't he make it mere hours without her? How could he crave her that desperately? He was about to climb the stairs when she appeared. The sight of her made him stagger back a step.

She wore a velvet dress with fur trim on the long sleeves and full skirt that brushed her calves. It was tight on her, pushing up the swell of her pert breasts in a way that had him stirring the moment she descended those steps. Everything about Lia was perfect. The glow of her golden skin, her long dark waves and muscular legs.

"Wow," he said, taking her hand and spinning her in place.

"Wow yourself." She ran her palms along his arms and looked at him with a carnal spark in her eyes.

After a few days of not having to dress for court, his red tailcoat was confining.

"You wore this that day," she said, toying with the gold embroidery, the medals he'd earned only in name pinned to the lapel. "I do hope you realize that it's red."

He growled playfully into her neck. "Yes, I realize it's red, and you have a bizarre fascination with turning me into that perverse—"

She shut him up with a kiss. Her palms smoothed his lapels, and he gathered her close, sweeping his tongue against hers.

"You're perfect," he said, and kissed her throat. He wanted to tear the dress right off her, but he'd already destroyed so many clothes. He had to believe the Guardian would return, and he had to believe that he'd find some way to replenish everything they had used.

For now, he had a banquet to attend.

They ate sitting on the furs around the tea table. Their plates heaped with turkey, a roasted beets, and walnut stuffing. For dessert they ate candied cherries straight from the jar. Although Alexander did stir a spoonful into his teacup of whisky.

"I'm sorry I can't give you a true banquet," he told her.

"This is perfect." She licked the dark red syrup from her fingertips. "Top three holidays."

He reached down and took her sticky finger in his mouth, sucking the remnants of the cherry flavor. "What are the other two?"

"Halloween '98. I got two pumpkins full of candy." She watched his confused expression and added, "I'll explain Halloween when we're home."

Home. The word struck something inside of him. He liked it. Home. Lia was home.

He refilled his whisky. "And the other?"

"New Year's '13. It's the first time I ever spent the holiday away from my family. I think I was rebelling against my dad's expectations. So I followed a waitress at the restaurant, and we rang in the New Year in Berlin, on a cold bridge, eating grapes and drinking champagne with hundreds of strangers. Also will explain that when we're home."

"I like when you say that," he told her. "Home. I want to learn about everything that makes you happy. I want to see everything through your eyes."

Lia sat up on her knees and pressed her nose to his. "I have a question."

He was too distracted by her scent, the tickle of her lashes on his cheeks, warmth that radiated from her. "Yes, my darling?"

"Why won't you come inside me?"

He sat back, and he wasn't sure if he should feel bewildered or amused at her sheer innocence. He wasn't sure if he should bend her over the settee and fuck her until she got the very thing she was asking for. Fuck, he needed inside of her.

He licked his lip and sipped his whisky because his mouth was dry from how much he *wanted*. "Pardon?"

A blush crept up her cheekbones. "You have your magic mushroom and I just wanted to know what it feels like. Why haven't you done it?"

"Because, Lia, you haven't asked me."

"Oh," she said, adjusting her hips, like she was all good and ready to grind on his cock. "Unless you don't want to."

Fuck, did he want to. Even thinking about filling her with his seed made him want to incinerate from the inside out. "My body is yours, remember? Ask what you will of me."

"I want you to come inside me." She nodded, pleased, and rubbing at his hard cock.

He pushed the table away and began to undo his cursed buttons. He hoped the mortal realm had clothes with decidedly fewer buttons. In fact, he'd simply live with no clothes on so that his insatiable little darling had instant access to his cock.

"I found something while you were cooking," she said.

His attention followed her to the crate he'd brought up from the cellar. She pulled out a fur-lined cloak the color of the dark cherries they were eating.

"That is a very old cloak."

"Exactly." Her lips were positively wicked as she smiled and said, "This is a Santa Claus cloak."

Alexander followed her train of thought. "No. Absolutely not. I won't."

She sat down on the corner of the settee with the cloak on her lap. Her pout was devastating, breasts half-moons rising and falling as she traced her finger across them. "Please. Pretty please. With cherries on top."

His cock reacted to her delicate whimper, the vulnerable sight of her. What did it say about him that he wanted to devour her like she was prey in his sights, a perfect gazelle in the woods? But the way he felt helpless to her desires, he knew, he knew that *he* was her prey.

"You know exactly what you're doing, Noelia Espinoza."

"What if I told you that since I met you sex with Santa Claus was on my list of sex fantasies?"

He loved that despite her confident words, her round cheeks were blushing. He loved that she dragged nervous fingers over her collar bone. And because he loved so many things about her, he couldn't deny her this. He might never be able to deny her anything.

And so, the spare heir of Saint Nikolas, last of his line, got up and donned the cloak. He growled low as he snapped the buckle at his throat. He would have felt utterly ridiculous if not for the devilish spark in her eyes.

Lia gasped her delight and pulled up the hem of her skirt to reveal the lace stockings that rested at her thighs. "Oh, yeah. You can come down my chimney anytime you want."

His heart pulsed a beat, and his blood sang a harmony. He prowled across the living room and came down to his knees in front of her. He parted her legs and lowered his face between her thighs. She tried to squeeze her legs shut, but he spread them farther. She wasn't wearing any underthings.

"You came ready for me."

She nodded eagerly. "What are you going to do about it?"

"Is this what you want?" he asked roughly, shoving his trousers down. Cock in hand, he nudged himself between her legs but didn't penetrate. He rocked against her wet heat. "You want to be fucked under the tree like a good little darling?"

"Yes," she moaned. "Please."

She reached down to guide him in. But he stepped just out of her reach, taking himself in hand with rough strokes.

"Too bad this cock is for naughty little darlings," he told her. "And you've been awfully good, Lia."

"Fuck, Alex," she sighed hard, then seeking her own pleasure with her fingers. "I can be naughty."

"Let me see," he ground out. "Let me see you touch your pretty little cunt."

The noises she made of surprise caused him to stroke himself again. She was too beautiful. Too much. He wasn't going to be able to stop himself from beating his dick senseless watching her bite her lower lip as she massaged the pink bead between her dark curls.

"Look at me," he said. "Look at me while you touch yourself."

She held his gaze as she tugged the front of her dress and freed one of her breasts. With her other hand, she slid one finger into her wet seam, glistening in the firelight.

"Come now, my darling. You can take more than that. You've had me inside you, after all."

"Like this?" She fucked herself with two fingers.

He rocked his head back and cursed at the ceiling. He was going to come undone. "Show me more."

She climbed up on her knees, resting on the curled ledge of the settee, lifting her dress up. She parted her knees just so, exposing her pink flesh, her fingers dripping with her sex. "Am I your naughty darling now?"

It was he who couldn't take it anymore, and the grin she flashed as he nearly crawled up behind her told him she knew that. She arched her back, wagging her perfect open heat and the pleated button of her ass at him. He gave her a long stroke of his tongue and held her in place as she whimpered and wriggled.

"Alex," she pleaded. "Fuck me."

"You're still too good," he cried out, grabbing hold of his dick. He was hard as diamonds.

"I'm not good. I've been fucking a stranger for days. I've let him come in my mouth, on my belly, and I'm about to let him come inside of me. I deserve to be spanked for that. Don't you think?"

Her wet folds were like a target. He palmed her ass and smoothed her perfect skin before landing the sharp crack of his palm.

She let loose a keening moan. "Yes, *yes*. Again."

He bunched up the hem of his tunic and buried his cock between her thighs, lining himself up with her wet slit. She rocked back against him, trying to angle him inside. The more she whimpered for him, the longer her denied her.

"You are a wicked little thing," he murmured, then clapped his hand on her backside, leaving the white imprint of his palm, there and then gone.

"Wicked enough to fuck?" she asked, glancing over her shoulder.

He ran fingers through her hair and pulled her head. He stole a long, passionate kiss, then caged her thighs with his legs. He guided the head of his cock at her entrance and swore they both stopped breathing. When he plunged inside and stretched her open, they shuddered together.

Her body arched back, and he pulsed into the tight heat of her channel.

"More, Alex. Please, I want more."

He gave it to her and drove harder, faster, easing back to swat her luscious ass. She reached her arm back to hold on to him, his own hand skating beneath the velvet dress to rub the swollen bead of her clit.

"You're mine, Lia." The words tumbled out in ragged pants. He was unravelling. Filling her with his need and desire. "There are still hundreds, thousands of ways I want to fuck you. Feel you this wet and willing and filthy for me."

"Only for you."

"Say it again," he said, desperate, driving harder, faster.

"Only for you," she cried.

"Yes, yes, *fuck*, Lia."

"Oh, God. I'm coming," she said. "I'm coming."

He banded an arm tighter around her waist as her pussy crashed around him. He relished every wave, kissed her tender throat as she rode out her pleasure.

When he pulled out of her, he ached.

"Come here." Stars danced in his vision as he sat back. He ran a fist over his sack and could barely think straight enough to say, "I want to look at you."

"Your turn," she said.

She straddled his thighs and impaled herself on his erection, still dripping with her orgasm. Every inch was agony, but he wanted it to be this way. He wanted to hold her against his chest and kiss her. He rocked slowly into her pussy, her sweet sighs exhaling against his lips. Sparks danced along his skin like the crackle of lightning, bright and thunderous, and then he was spilling inside her, pulsing his hips until he spent every drop.

Lia kissed his temples, his jaw, his mouth. "I don't think I'll ever get tired of this."

He caught her hard nipple between his teeth and delighted in the little yelp she made. He smoothed his bite with tender licks that made her sink against him. "I'll make sure you never get tired of this."

"Promise?"

Alexander had broken several promises and oaths. His sworn oath to his brother had resulted in his death. He'd made a promise, long before that, to his cousin Kit, and the memory of that night still shamed him. He wanted to tell her no—that he'd find a way to disappoint her because that was who he was. But she'd told him that he could choose. He could choose to be someone different. Better. For her.

"I promise," he said, and he felt the words stitch themselves into his heart.

THAT NIGHT when Alexander went to sleep with Lia tucked tightly against his body, he dreamt. It was always the same memory. The recurring nightmare of that day, long ago.

The woods were dark, but the moon was a beam overhead. Branches reached out, caressing the boy like slender fingers.

"Kit?" Alexander asked.

They'd gone too deep into the heart of the forest. They'd strayed into the winding paths of ancient trees. When night fell and they tumbled into the mouth of a pit, the laughter from the two boys turned into screams.

"*I can climb up,*" Alexander said. *He was the tallest of the two and was accustomed to scaling turrets and walls.* "*I'll get help.*"

"*Please,*" Kit had whispered.

This time, when Alexander replayed the memory he thought he'd buried long ago, his cousin's pale shoulders were outlined by a single stroke of moonlight. And when he turned around, his eyes were rimmed with flame.

19
LIA

Lia was too wired to sleep. She lay in bed with Alexander, admiring the dips of his abdomen, the trail of hair that led to his cock. Everything about him was brutal. From his muscles to the scars he had earned in all the stories he'd told her of running around the kingdom. His eyes fluttered restlessly, and she pressed a soft kiss to his temple, hoping that he wasn't having a nightmare.

She must have snoozed at some point because light trickled from the edges of the curtains. A feeling sank in her belly. It was too early to be so bright. She checked her phone, and it still read four in the morning. The days had blended together—from the snowstorm to the shadow sylph to the Northern Lights and the devilbane. It might just be that their Christmas Eve had been their most normal day together.

Lia curled back on her side, listening to the creaking sound of the house. Once she noticed the tiny sounds of the groaning wood beams and how loud the silence was, she couldn't unnotice it. With sleep evading her, she made a mental list of what they'd have to do once they got back into town. It was silly, but she wished she had her travel stationery. The notebook and bright colored pens and washi tape she always packed. Her fingers itched to write down a new list.

Alexander was all it would say at the top of the page. Because she couldn't help herself, she'd decorate it with illustrations of devilbane and a tiny Christmas tree. And what would follow? Angry winter prince? Huge cock? Body by woodchopping? Then there were the other things—

Sweet
Patient
Caring
Insecure
Passionate
Insatiable
Devastatingly sexy
Love.

She highlighted the word in her mind and drew obnoxious hearts around it. The last time she'd done something like that had been in high school, and her crush had broken her heart by throwing away her Valentine's Day card in front of everyone. She was long past her teenage years, and she'd lost hope of finding someone who made her feel the way Alexander did.

But love?

How could she love him? She didn't know him. Gracie liked to say that she needed to go out with someone on four dates, separated by one-week intervals, before she could have sex with them, and twelve months before she could call it love. Helena hit it and quit it. No attachments. Their parents had met in college and then immigrated to New Jersey where they got married and got busy having a family, a restaurant, and a neat, orderly life. Their love was wrought over decades of hard work.

Was there even a *right* way to fall in love? And besides, her cousin Maria had known her husband for four years, and they still got divorced after six months of marriage. Meanwhile, her high school best friend met a girl in Dublin during a five-day educational trip and literally never left the country. Six years later, she was happily married and enjoying the best butter and beer in the world.

Lia wished she had her sisters with her. That was the thought she took with her as she fell back into a dark sleep. But in her dreams, there was howling and a dark forest. Red eyes. Nightbirds. Someone crying.

When she woke again, her heart hammered at her throat. Slowly, a hand wrapped around her waist. Alexander pinned her against his torso, groaning awake as he pressed his erection to the small of her back. Just like that, any memory of the strange Brother's Grimm fairytale vanished. She hooked her leg around his, giving him access to her entrance, and he plunged inside her with long, languid thrusts until they chased each other's orgasms.

"I definitely had morning sex on my list," she said, her voice still raspy with sleep.

When she sat up, she did a double take. All it took was one look at her face, and Alexander shot up, alert. "What's wrong?"

She blinked and blinked. She rubbed her eyes, hoping it was just her being drunk from so much sex, if that was even possible. But no, she was seeing him correctly. Two thick stripes of silver ran from his temples, like a crown. She wasn't sure if he looked like a young sexy Santa or like a hot villain in a spy movie.

"Your hair," she said.

Alexander picked up the foggy mirror on the bedside table. "What in the name of the Saint?"

She didn't know what to say, only dressed quickly. "Have you ever seen that happen before?"

He shook his head and set the mirror down. Unlike the other times he'd noticed something abnormal, he didn't get angry. Instead, he was deadly still, more resigned. Something was wrong. Neither of them could deny it anymore.

"We must go," he said. The fear in his voice made her hurry.

Lia dressed in her clothes from the day she got lost. Even though they fit, it was like they belonged to someone else.

Alexander packed up leftover turkey in jars and the bottle of whisky, though she hoped they would reach the town before they had to use it to keep warm. They straightened out the house, made sure the fireplace was extinguished, and tugged on boots and coats.

Lia glanced at her phone. Still no service, but she wanted to look at her lock screen. At her sisters' faces.

"I won't let anything happen to you, Lia." Alexander brushed his fingers against her cheek. His smile was strained. "Saint Nikolas was the saint of travelers, too."

"I know." She squeezed his hand.

He used a hammer to undo the nail he'd wedged through the door. When it opened, snow slid in at their feet like a small avalanche, but at least they could see the forest. She gathered that it was shin-deep.

"I'll make a path, and you follow, all right?"

She remembered her favorite stories from school. She'd thought they were so romantic once. Orpheus leading Eurydice out of the underworld. Only when she got older and revisited those stories, she realized he'd been an idiot. He hadn't trusted their love. He hadn't trusted her and lost her again. Lia and Alexander were nothing like that story, but something about the way he cast one last glance at her sent a prickle of trepidation down her spine.

As he cleared a path for them, she followed. The forest

surrounding them was pristine, dusted with several inches of fresh powder still falling.

But when she looked up to let the snowflakes kiss her cheeks, she realized the snow was all around her—frozen still.

"Alex," she said in warning.

Alexander stopped. A muscle moved at his jaw as his frown deepened. Flurries were suspended on their way to the ground. He reached out his hand, and they melted on the surface of his coat. His eyes snapped up to the trees where a squirrel was petrified mid-air on its way to the next branch. An owl's feathers flared in a wide wingspan.

"No," Alexander said. "No, this cannot—"

He trudged through the snow, and she followed, cutting a path around the cabin. Lia expected to find more animals frozen —instead the sight was more startling.

There, in the clearing beside the house, was a reindeer. His reindeer. Kilian. Utterly and completely frozen, his forelegs rearing at the body in front of him. The man in the snow had short golden hair, a sun-kissed tan, and a lavish, golden version of Alexander's frock. Both of their faces were twisted in absolute horror.

Lia staggered back when she saw it. At first, the shadow melted into the dark spindly trees, but as she took several steps away, she saw the awful sight: a giant shadow sylph in the shape of a tarantula with glowing white eyes and furry pincers. A long thread of ooze spilled from its mouth, and that's when she realized. The ooze was moving. Super slowly.

The falling snow wasn't *frozen* but moving at the most micro speed. She whirled on Alexander.

"You slowed down time." She touched her hand to her lips. "Don't you see? Your magic is doing this."

"No. It was supposed to be *over*." Alexander shook his head, threading fingers along the hair that had turned silver overnight.

His face crumpled with guilt and terror and something worse. The realization that it wasn't over. He squeezed his arm, right where he knew the Mark of the Saint had stopped along with time.

She went to him, but he held her back. "Alex. Talk to me."

"Go inside, Lia."

"*No.*"

"Please, Lia. I will fix this. But you have to stand back."

He was so anguished, she did as he asked and put a wide berth between her and the frozen sight before them.

Alexander climbed up on the back of the shadow sylph. As he wrapped his arms around the creature's neck, she felt a tug at the back of her belly button, a pressure in her ears, like the world was screaming, sighing, pushing upstream.

And then, a release.

The owl flew. The squirrel finished leaping to the next branch. A breeze pushed flurries all around like the inside of an upturned snow globe. The reindeer neighed and stomped, while the man crawled away.

And then there was Alexander—he screamed as the spider came to life, eight hairy legs trying to unsaddle him. With a loud crunch, the spider went limp, melting and dissipating like the first shadow beast they'd killed.

Alexander hauled himself onto his knees, breathing hard.

Her phone came alive, dozens of messages and missed calls surging to alert her that even though they had spent three days, three glorious days together, it was still December 21st. Her message to her sisters finally went through. She hurried to type more, to let them know she was alive, but the battery chose that moment to die.

None of that mattered because as the day caught up to them, so did the markings on Alexander's arm. He screamed as the Mark spread, this time starting at his other hand to mirror the left. Inky black runes and ivy patterns vanished up his sleeve, burning their way. He screamed and screamed and sank to his knees. She wanted to go to him, but the blonde man got there first.

Lia cried out as the stranger kicked Alexander across the face. "You selfish bastard."

"Stop!" Lia crossed the distance, and as the man turned to see where the scream had come from, she swung with all her strength and popped him in the face. Pain shot up her arm, but it was worth it to hear a crack.

He cupped his bloody nose. "You wretched little—"

"I wouldn't finish that sentence, Hansel." Alexander rubbed his jaw as he got back to his feet.

"Your brother?" Lia repeated, cradling her fist to her chest.

Alexander stood between them, his body acting as a shield. "Lia Espinoza. Meet my brother, Hansel Nikolas, Master of Alchemy and Royal Dick."

"You have royal dicks?" she whispered, but thankfully, he hadn't heard her.

She couldn't see her beautiful Alexander in Hansel's cold, regal face.

The man sneered, casting a disgusted glance at the reindeer before returning his anger to Alexander. "You've outdone yourself now, brother. Out of all the utter idiotic things you've done in your life—"

"Why are you here, Hans?"

"Isn't it obvious? I have come to bring you home."

20

ALEXANDER

Home, Alexander repeated in his mind. Home was this cabin. Home was whatever place Lia was going to ferry him away to because he wanted his home to be with her.

"No," Alexander said. He kept saying that word. Kept hoping that the truth was anything but. That he hadn't *frozen* time for three days. He felt the Mark working its way to his heart.

"What do you mean, no?" Hans sputtered. Then winced. The shadow spider had slashed through his sleeve. "I hate what you've done to your hair, by the by."

Alexander grunted. He felt about his brother the way he did about kidney pie. A general dislike. But he'd already lost one brother, and the kingdom needed someone, even if it wasn't Alexander. He'd convince Hans to return. It had been days for Alexander but not for the world out there.

"Get inside. I'll take a look at your disfigured face."

He pressed a kiss to Lia's cheek, and her knuckles. He hadn't had a moment to tell her how fiercely his love for her had doubled upon seeing her crack Hans's septum.

"Very well," the Golden Prince of the Eternal Winter Forest said.

As Hans and Lia went inside, Alexander rested his forehead to his reindeer's. Kilian huffed and shook his mane. "I know. I know, old friend. But your oath to me is done."

Kilian responded with a stomp and a huff, then remained sentry at the door of the cabin.

Back inside, Hans surveyed the living room like he'd rather take his chances with a shadow sylph than touch anything.

Hans wrinkled his nose. "What is that smell?"

"Sex. I know you're not used to it," Alexander said, removing his coat and tunic to examine the Mark. Both sides had spread, encroaching toward his heart. He wanted to retch and scream and break something. But then he looked at Lia, worrying her bottom lip, and he knew he had to find the strength to get through it.

Hans rolled his pale blue eyes. "You waste no time."

"What do you want, Hansel?" Alexander said.

"I would like some tea, Alexander, rosehip, two sugars. You weren't raised by barbarian woodlings, no matter how much you acted like it."

"You have some nerve," Lia said. "Coming here and—"

"*I* have the nerve?" Hans interrupted, pressing his fingers to his chest like he was the injured party. "The king was murdered, *our brother* murdered, and my dearest Alexander runs. I had hoped you'd prove Father wrong, but you're a waste, to the very end."

"I don't think I broke his nose enough," Lia said, and Alexander stopped her before she could rush his brother. He adored her fierce protectiveness. Lia, who drew hearts in the foggy glass of the bathing room mirror, and loved her tree decorations, and marveled every time she'd witnessed magic. She was protective of him. No one had protected him before.

He hated that his brother was here, ruining their plans. He hated that his own magic had been the reason they'd been stuck inside the cabin and kept her from her family. Now he had to use that power to heal his brother. He rolled up his sleeves and sat beside Hans.

"Do you want me to heal you or not?" Alexander asked through gritted teeth.

"Very well. You need the practice." Hans winced as he shoved off his tailcoat. The shadow sylph had left a single stripe, but it didn't look infected with poison. Alexander couldn't very well let him walk around with an open bloody gash. Hadn't he loathed his own father when he refused to grant the miracles of pleading villagers? He hadn't hesitated when it came to Lia? What kind of man did that make him?

Alexander let the magic of the Mark course through him, pulsing in a glow that stitched the skin of the wound together.

"Right," Hans said, peering up at Alexander with guarded awe. Never had a man looked as uncomfortable uttering the words "Thank you" as Hansel did in that moment. "And my nose?"

He placed his thumb and index finder over his brother's broken ridge. As Hans closed his eyes, Alexander snapped the fracture back in place.

Hans let out a hoarse howl. "You bloody sadist!"

"Oh, it'll give you character. Now, what do want?" Alexander asked, moving to Lia's side on the settee. "I told you I wanted no part of this. You are the second son. You rule."

"Believe me, if there was another way, I would seek it. But alas. You are the only hope we have to stop Celeste." He looked around the room, noticing that it appeared lived in. "Honestly, brother. I require tea. I've had a very long day."

"Days," Alexander corrected, then explained how he had stretched out time for three days.

THE HEART OF WINTER

"I see." Hans licked his canine and smoothed down the front of his tunic. "Then I will require something far stronger."

Lia opened her satchel and withdrew the whisky bottle. Alexander hurried into the kitchen for three teacups. He stopped himself from spitting in his brother's and set them down on the table. Lia filled each one with a generous pour, her fingers trembling as she pushed the cork back into the neck.

Hans picked up his teacup and grimaced at the chip that marred his. "Long live the Saint."

Alexander and Lia didn't repeat the words but tapped their teacups to his.

As he drank, Alexander was overcome with the feeling that Hans didn't belong here. His brother, despite having trekked across the Hallowed Path and survived an attack from the shadow sylph, clearly with Kilian's help, had not a hair out of place. The golden curl that flopped at the center of his forehead was intentional.

"Why am I the only hope of stopping Celeste?" Alexander asked. "If she wants me so badly, why can't I let this cursed power free?"

"Because," Hans said tersely. "There has always been a Nikolas. There will always *be* a Nikolas. We are the shepherds of this legacy, and you have the strength to fight back against Celeste's intent to destroy everything we have built."

"I don't understand," Alexander said. "Why is she doing this? Why can't you stop her?"

"I do not know!" He spilled whisky on his tunic, choking the air like he wished it was Alexander's throat. "If I could, I would but I can't."

Lia, who'd been sitting quietly, leaned forward. "He's hiding something."

Hans's blue eyes settled on her. They were the color of the sky after the first snow fall. Cold and endless. He arched an eyebrow, and Alexander saw what his brother saw. Her high cheekbones and burnished skin. The perfect bow of her lips and the wild waves that tumbled over her shoulders.

"I see what triggered your power, Alexander. Though, a *human*, really?"

"Careful, brother."

"What do you mean triggered his power?" Lia asked.

"You wielded the power of time," Hans said, using his own palm as a saucer. When he glanced at the tree and noticed the tiny Santa Claus trinket, he grimaced. "Not even father was able to do that. Clearly all the magic you used took a toll on you, which explains your hair. It's growing on me, by the way."

"No one *asked* you," Lia muttered.

"And you, a mere mortal, have no say in this. Even if you are the reason my dear brother's power awakened so spectacularly." Alexander loathed to admit Hans was right, but he was. Alexander had felt it. When his power had gone wild and Lia had calmed him with her kiss. The world had gone still, eerily quiet. But he'd been too consumed with her, too blissfully relieved that he'd outrun his own curse that he hadn't stopped to realize that it had been a dream.

A dream. Perhaps the magic was the reason he'd had those nightmares. Though it didn't matter. The world had caught up to them, and there was nowhere for him to hide.

Han took another sip. "Don't fight this, Alexander. You will claim the rest of the blessing, and you will ascend to your place as Saint Nikolas."

"Hey, you," Lia said.

"Me?" Hans tapped his chest. No one talked to him that way, and as much as his revulsion was clear, he also sparked with interest. Alexander growled with possessive anger.

Lia rested a hand on his thigh. "Yeah, I'm talking to you. You are the Master of Alchemy, is that right?"

Hans preened as he sipped. "That I am."

"That's it?"

Alex wasn't sure what she was getting at. She already knew that.

"What do you mean *that's it*?" Hans scoffed. "I possess the power to turn lead to gold, to transform elements at their very core. I am the keeper of the eternal mysteries that your small human life couldn't begin to encompass. I know the secrets of the past, the heart of our kingdom."

"Secrets?" Lia rolled her eyes. "Your boring little utopia? Alexander told me everything. Nothing ever happens except solstices and orgies? Yawn. You've never been to my town, pretty boy."

"I'd say that's quite a lot to keep track of." Hans sat up, his shoulders tense, defensive.

What was she doing? But she only brushed her finger over the top of his knee, and he knew to let her finish.

"Whatever." She drank deep from her cup. "There's nothing about your kingdom that's remotely interesting. Alexander says you don't even have a dungeon. What's your biggest secret? A sugar cookie recipe?"

Hans sat forward so quickly, whisky sloshed down his hand. He pressed a finger to his temple. "You have *no* idea what lies beneath our palace. We may not have a dungeon, but we do have the caverns, and if Alexander does not complete the Mark of the Saint it will—"

Hans coughed hard, then caught himself, shocked at the words he'd revealed.

"What caverns?" Alexander asked.

"You're cleverer than you look," Hans said, but neither Lia nor Alexander took the bait. "Enough of this, brother. Come *home*."

"And you clearly hate my world. But you came all this way,

put your manicured little haircut at risk to get back the brother you dishonor."

"He dishonors this family every day."

"Why?" she asked. "You're lying. You know what happens if he doesn't complete the Mark. So just tell him."

"I should not *need* to tell him anything. Alexander needs to do his duty to his kingdom, to his bloodline." Hans shook his head. "If the Mark wasn't so clearly embedded into your skin, I'd have believed Father's suspicion that you were a bastard."

The words were a slap. Alexander was filled with rage he hadn't felt in days. The hatred at his kin, at himself, all came flooding back. A bastard. Was that why his father had been so cruel?

Alexander got to his feet. "We're leaving."

"Wait! I didn't mean it," Hans said, hurrying to calm Alexander. "I'm sorry. I've been frozen for three days, and this mortal dares speak to me this way— Please, Alexander."

"Why won't you tell me?" Alexander asked darkly.

"I *can't*." Hans pressed his lips together and made a frustrated sound. He drank, fingers trembling around the teacup. "Even if I wanted to, I physically cannot tell you what is in those caverns."

"If you can't, who can?" Lia asked.

Hans shook his head. For the first time, Alexander noticed the shadows under his brother's eyes. "Our kingdom was designed this way. The king commands, uses his powers to maintain order and peace. The Master of Alchemy ensures the kingdom never wants for anything and maintains knowledge. Secrets. Secrets that will burn a hole in my throat if I utter them."

Alexander straightened. Hans was many things. Arrogant. Selfish. Vain. Spoiled. But he didn't lie. Not when the truth could cause more pain and mischief.

"Listen to me, Alexander. I know you hate our kingdom, but if the Eternal Winter Forest falls, if there is not a Saint Nikolas to rule, you have no idea the terror that will be unleashed and it won't stop at our borders. It will spread. If you care about anyone, your mortal lover, this realm, this shabby burrow, then you'll come home and do the right thing."

The right thing.

"When have you known me to do the right thing?" Alexander asked.

Hans drained his teacup. "You have it in you. I know it."

It was that kindness, that small belief that Alexander could do anything but cause ruination, that told him his wretched golden brother was serious.

Alexander turned to Lia. He had promised he'd protect her. He had promised so many things. But how could he lead her into his world when he didn't know what he'd find? His brother's murderer was waiting. What darkness would threaten his realm, and this one? What if Lia was used as a pawn? What if he lost her? What if he was losing her now? And what if he'd never had her to begin with? After all, their three days together had been a miracle of time. Stolen. Fabricated. All while the rest of the world was trapped under his spell.

Wretched. Selfish. He was no better than when she'd met him.

The realization that he had to leave her shattered him. Worst of all, he had to find the strength to not break apart. Lia was his strength.

"Then let us go, brother."

Hans slackened with relief and then drained his teacup. "Leave the mortal behind. She'll only get in the way."

"Like Hell. I'm not letting him go alone at some cryptic prince's word. Do you know how many fantasy books I've read?"

Hans licked his canine, his patience thin. "You will only be used *against* my brother."

"Enough!" Alexander barked, tugging on his tunic. He shoved Hans toward the door. He ground out, "Let's go. Now."

Hans tumbled out of the threshold, Alexander at his heel.

"Protect her. Get her back home," Alexander said to Kilian, who guarded the entrance. The reindeer bowed, acknowledging Alexander's oath.

Behind him, Lia was pulling on her coat. Her cheeks were flushed from drinking too fast. She moved like a bee in a garden, making sure she hadn't forgotten anything. Checking off some list in her mind. She smiled at him, and that's how he wanted to remember her. His light, his sunshine in the terrible dark of his heart.

"I love you, Noelia Espinoza." Alexander raised his fists, and devilbane shot through the floorboards, thick and full of thorns, at the threshold. They crisscrossed like a gate, barring her way out.

"Alex!" she cried out, reaching out for him. Then she winced as she pricked herself on the vines.

That's what it felt like as he closed the door in her face. Like there were thorns around his heart, too, because he *was* a wretched man to leave the woman he loved. To leave her willingly because it was the only way to keep her safe.

Lia's cries echoed from inside the cabin, and he knew they would haunt him with every step that led him back to where he'd started. Back to the Eternal Winter Forest.

21
LIA

Alexander.

Lia yelled his name more times than she wanted to count. She yelled it until her voice hurt. She yelled his name one last time to make sure that she could hear it, that it had been real and she hadn't imagined him.

Of course it had been real. She could still feel the effects of him on her body, the soreness that pulsed between her legs, the splinters in her heart because he was gone.

He'd left her.

He'd told her that he loved her and still left.

Lia imagined having Alexander say those words, words she was too afraid to speak herself, would have been a moment of joy. Instead, her heart was splintered, cracking like fragile glass.

For a long moment, she sat there in front of the door made of devilbane and thorns. She stared at the shimmering silver berries, the feathering leaves that still bore dirt from the ground through which they'd sprouted. Alexander had done that. He'd used the magic he so loathed to trap her.

I love you, Noelia Espinoza.

Noelia Espinoza, the girl he'd met on that icy lake, might

have accepted being left behind. But something had happened when she'd emerged from the ice. She was stronger. Herself, only more. And so, Lia searched the cabin for the knife and began cutting the vines. Thorns drew blood from slender cuts. They were too thick. She tried to open the windows, but it was like the whole house was keeping her prisoner.

"You fucking asshole!" she yelled, and Lia wasn't certain if she meant Alexander or his pompous idiot brother. It was Hans's fault they were apart.

She bit down on her trembling lip. She would not cry. She couldn't. She let her anger course through her, then fuel her body. Lia took a steadying breath. He wouldn't let her starve, so there *had* to be a way out. She was wondering if the chimney might be big enough for her to scale, when the door swung open and let in a burst of cold wind.

"Alexander?" Hope flooded her voice as she cut to the threshold.

It wasn't her love. It was a tall man, perhaps in his mid-twenties. He had pale skin with a green undertone and sharp eyes the color of new leaves. His hair was long, brown, and tangled. He was haphazardly dressed in trousers and an untucked tunic.

"Lia," he said, holding his palms up.

She took a step back, reaching for her knife again. For once she was grateful that the vines created a barrier of protection. But as he approached, they receded, uncurling and slithering back into the ground beneath the floorboards.

Fuck.

"Who are you?"

"Lia," he repeated. "I mean you no harm. I am—"

"How do you know my name?"

He remained, barefoot in the snow on the other side of the threshold.

"I am Kilian, sworn knight to Prince Alexander."

She knew that name but— No. She shook her head. Saints, magic tattoos, shadow monsters—fine. But this, *this* might be the thing that tipped her over, past the looking glass and into a world she truly couldn't fathom. "Kilian? Like his reindeer?"

A smile tugged at his lips. "This must be a bit of a shock to your kind."

"Mortal ordinary human?" She nodded, panic hitching her voice into a shrieking soprano. "Okay. Okayokayokayokay. You're a shapeshifter?"

Kilian chuckled. The sound too playful for the distress she was going through. "Elfenhörn."

"Elfenhörn?" she asked. "I thought that was a forest."

"Yes, but who do you think dwells in the forest?" He stepped into the cabin, and she let him walk right past her. He picked up the whisky bottle. But instead of drinking from it, he corked it. He offered Lia a smile so beautiful, she felt dazed. Was everyone from that world ethereal? "In case the ride to your village gets too cold."

Lia processed what the shapeshifting reindeer had just said to her. "We're going after Alex. You're his *knight*. You can't believe he's safe with Prince Goldilocks, do you?"

"My apologies, Lady Lia. But my orders stand. Alexander wants you returned to your family."

"I'm not a package that needs to be delivered. He knows that." She finger-combed her hair and had the urge to tug. "What if I never see him again? What if he's walking into danger? What if he's—" *Fuck*, she thought. *What if he's hurt or worse?* The tears finally caught up to her. "There has to be a different solution than Alexander sacrificing his entire life on the word of a brother who treated him horribly."

"Ah, but he isn't doing it for Hans," Kilian said somberly. "He's doing it for you. It's his choice."

"What about my choice?" she whispered.

After all, they'd chosen each other first. He'd chosen her first. She was ready to follow him into the unknown. But there she stood, alone in the cabin that had been their retreat from the outside. Now it was just empty rooms, a cold fireplace, a wilting tree. She craved his touch, his warmth. She needed closeness.

She needed her sisters.

Lia met Kilian's leaf-green eyes. She relented. "Take me back."

Kilian nodded once then guided her out of the cabin, this time closing the door for good.

And then Kilian started stripping off his tunic.

"Oh," Lia said, and turned to give him privacy. She caught the smooth expanse of lean muscles just before she faced the snow-covered trees.

"So, are all Elfenhörn reindeer shifters?" She winced at her words. Nervous chit-chat was not one of her strengths.

She heard the rustle of clothes being shoved into something. A satchel, perhaps.

"Elfenhörn were many things once," he said. "But that is a story for another time. For now, tell me where we are going."

Lia's thoughts were moving faster than she could process. But she concentrated enough to remember the address of the inn in Baden-Baden. "How's your sense of direction?"

"It's been decades since I've traveled through this realm, but I believe I'll manage."

Decades? He looked about Gracie's age. It was another thing to add to the holiday wonderland that was her life since the snowstorm.

"You can turn around now," Kilian said.

Lia heard the change before she could face him. Heard the crack of bone, the pained sigh he released. The wind whistled, and the ground moved where hooves stomped. Where the beautiful knight had been was the majestic reindeer who had helped save her life.

She approached slowly, and he tapped his cold nose to her palm, then snuffed at the saddle half-buried in the snow.

"Right," she said. One summer of horseback riding lessons had cured her of wanting to be a horse girl. But at least she could saddle up, tugging on the leathers and buckles that fit perfectly on his frame.

When she was finished, Lia climbed up and grabbed the reins. She gave a final longing glance at the cabin. The forest that had enveloped her, protected her like a creature hibernating until it was time to emerge.

The time was now.

KILIAN TROTTED SWIFTLY through the snow as trees became a blur. When she thought they were going too fast, she shut her eyes. But what she saw behind her eyelids was Alexander. Alexander haloed by stars and devilbane. Alexander consuming her body, devouring her heart.

I love you.

She didn't get to say it back.

She blinked cold tears that turned to ice.

Lia lost track of time, but it was still daylight when they trudged out of the forest and into a Christmas market. The same market where she'd gotten lost. Onlookers stared at the woman riding the reindeer, like it was part of the show. Children scuttled in groups to get closer, and adults muttered in angry German. Though to be fair, Lia thought everything in German sounded a touch angry.

"Straight across and make a left," she said as they eased to a trot.

Lia waved and pulled her hood over her eyes as she saw people recording her. She could not be a Christmas holiday meme. Sword and sorcery she could handle. The internet she could not.

Kilian turned on a single road, cars slowing down behind them. As they got closer to the inn, Lia scrambled for what she would say. Would she look different to them? She felt different in so many ways. To her sisters it had been less than a day since Lia went missing. Meanwhile, Lia's whole life had been turned inside out.

When the small inn appeared with its gingerbread house windows and chocolate trim, Lia's relief and anxiety were at war.

"I won't tell them," she decided.

Her family was superstitious. Her grandmother was staunchly Catholic but read tarot and decoded dreams. But that kind of every day magic was different than the literal magic she'd been witness to. Who was to say her sisters would even believe her? Perhaps it would be like the time she made a pretend boyfriend named Joshua in high school and they saw through the lie in ten seconds?

In the small yard decorated with three-foot statues of lumberjack Santas smoking pipes and manic-looking reindeer with red noses, they came to a stop. Lia hopped off the saddle. The surrounding area was quiet, and the car was gone.

Lia went over her plan. She'd sneak in while her sisters were away, try to charge her phone and call them.

Good plan.

Solid plan.

But when Kilian shifted back into human form and stood before her, naked as the sun was hot, she did not expect the scream that followed.

"What the actual fuck?" Helena thundered behind her.

Lia whirled around. "Hey!"

Helena and Gracie crowded at the back door, dressed in fashionable leather boots and peacoats. Helena cocked her eyebrow at Kilian, who was shamelessly still standing naked. Gracie cast her eyes down, her blush radioactive and made worse by the cold.

Helena stammered. Lia had never heard her sister stammer. "He just—did he just—"

"I just did," Kilian said, and Lia almost wondered if he loved the attention. He unhooked the satchel from the saddle and used it to cover his sizable dick, which she was admirably trying to not look at.

"This is Kilian. He's—" Lia couldn't finish the lie.

"I believe we should get inside?" Kilian whispered, his words turning into little clouds.

"You think?" Helena said, opening the door.

They filed into the cozy kitchen. Being back there was surreal. It was like she was physically there but the rest of her was in the cabin, with Alexander. Still, Lia managed to take off her boots and coat at the door.

By the time they sat down around the wooden breakfast table, Kilian had finished tugging on his clothes. He quickly made himself at home sitting beside Gracie and offering her a small bow.

"Noelia Luz Espinoza Peralta, you have so much explaining to do," Helena seethed. Her husky voice boomed in that way she got when she was mad, or excited, or passionate, or...Helena was just loud.

"I can explain."

"Oh, you'll explain. But first I have to murder you for making us worry all night. Then I'll resurrect you." She stomped around the kitchen and pulled Lia into a bone crushing hug.

Lia let go of a sob trapped in her chest. She inhaled Helena's lavender perfume, the orange scent of her favorite shampoo. Gracie's hand closed around Lia's, and for the first time since she entered those doors, Lia remembered that her life had been waiting for her. Guilt made her sob harder until she let it all out.

Helena let her go and pulled four glasses from the open kitchen shelves. Kilian withdrew the bottle of whisky from the satchel and offered it to her.

"Might as well," Helena said, plopping down at the table with a hard sigh as she poured the whisky. "Where the hell have you been?"

She started with the truth. "I got lost on a trail leading from the market."

"When we couldn't find you we tried to ping your location," Gracie said. Her voice was soft, grounding. "But the blue dot kept moving. We drove for hours trying to chase it."

"Then we got stuck in a ditch off the side of a road," Helena added, grimacing as she took a sip. "We got a ride back by a farmer slash mandolin player who wanted to marry Gracie."

"He did not," Gracie pouted. "Anyway, when you didn't show, we went to file a missing person's report, but we were told to go to the nearest embassy, and that's what we were doing when we got your text but you weren't responding. We were going to go looking for you and then you two showed up."

"If you were hooking up, you should have just texted us." Helena's wide, sultry lips twisted into a grin. "We spent all night and all morning worried sick, and you were with Rudolph the Well-hung Reindeer? Also, details."

No one spoke, which made the sound of Gracie nearly choking on her whisky and Kilian clapping her back to help clear her airways that much louder.

"Oh, I'm really quite average for an Elfenhörn," Kilian assured Helena with a wink.

"I'm sorry, but you're taking all of this very well," Lia said.

"I'm not," Gracie said, breathing fast and shallow.

"What *is* this?" Helena asked, gesticulating with her hands like she did when she got agitated. "And why do I feel like I've run a marathon? My legs are killing me."

"Ah," Kilian said. "That would be the effect from Alexander slowing time."

"Who the fuck is Alexander?" Helena asked.

"I haven't been gone since yesterday," Lia said. "I mean I have, but for me it was three days..."

She told them about the breakup call with George, the snowstorm. Alexander piercing the space between their worlds with Kilian. Falling through the lake. He'd saved her, and they'd survived. She told them about what she knew of the Eternal Winter Forest, their hunt, and living on turkey and wrinkled root vegetables and booze. She told them they were going to search for the market, but that's when they realized Alexander had stretched time nearly to a stop. And they didn't interrupt her. Not once. Which was a miracle on its own.

"Then he left with his brother," Lia said.

She didn't miss the way Kilian's upper lip twitched at the mention of Hans. She hoped Kilian hated Hans, too.

"Okay, I need a minute," Helena said.

"We have to call Mom and Dad," Gracie added.

Lia smacked her forehead. "Did you tell them I was missing?"

"Fuck no." Helena laughed incredulously. "I didn't need them getting on the first flight here trying to find their way to the German forest. We told them that you had diarrhea and were sleeping it off."

"Hells," Lia said, nearly choking on her drink. "Come on."

"Would you rather we have told the truth?"

Lia grumbled but conceded.

"I'm going to place an order to the one pizza place in town," Gracie said.

Helena scoffed. "You must be starving if you were eating quail eggs and grass and shit."

Lia rolled her eyes. She wanted to correct her, but then Helena leaned in, resting her chin on her fists. Lia knew the look of mischief.

"What did you and that prince guy do for three whole days?" Helena asked.

Lia knew her blush betrayed her. She'd conveniently left that part out. It was hers and Alexander's. She tried to stare-contest her sister into submission, but Helena had the best poker face and didn't blink.

"You totally lost your v-card to Santa Claus's grandson!"

Gracie did her best to stifle a laugh but failed.

"He's actually Saint Nikolas's great-great...." Kilian began.

"I think they got that part," Lia assured him with a gentle pat of his hand.

He refilled everyone's drinks. Gracie called the pizza place, and placed an order in her terrible broken German. Lia was so hungry, even non-New York pizza sounded like the most amazing thing in the world.

When Gracie returned to her seat, she glanced at Kilian, then at Lia. Something seemed to dawn in her wide, brown eyes.

"Oh my God," Gracie said softly. "I just realized. Slowing down time makes sense. How else would the real Santa Claus deliver all those presents in one day?"

Helena laughed. "The *real* Santa?"

"Can we not?" Lia buried her face in her arms.

"So you're not marrying George?" Helena asked. "I just need clarification since your Christmas boo is gone."

Lia shook her head. "No. I'm not marrying George. Even if

I hadn't met Alexander, I wouldn't have changed my mind when we got back home."

Helena came up behind her and kissed her younger sister on the top of her head. "Good. That's what we were hoping. But you had to arrive to that place on your own. Plus, if you'd have married him, I would have poisoned him on your wedding night for being rude to me."

"Helena!" Gracie said, scandalized.

"I mean like laxatives in his drink, calm down."

"That feels like a faulty strategy," Kilian said, licking his bottom lip. "You'd need something stronger, like witch's bane."

Helena turned her attention to Kilian. It was like she was noticing him for the first time. She sat back down and studied him. In another life, Helena would have made a good interrogator, which was a frightening thought. Instead, she was a lawyer who worked pro-bono for women in domestic abuse situations and the kind of disputes that never made the headlines but had the potential to change someone's life.

Helena gestured her drink at him. "What about you?"

"What about me?" Kilian asked.

"You're Alexander's knight? What does that mean?"

Kilian took a swallow, eyes flicking from sister to sister. "It's a long story, for another time. But Alexander released me from my vow. I am free to go anywhere."

"Where will you go?" came Gracie's shy question.

"I suppose—" Kilian sat forward, turning to only answer Gracie. "Home. Lia is safe. My vow might be complete, but Alexander is still my friend, and whatever is happening there, I must go to his side."

"Great," Helena said. "We're going with you."

It was Lia's turn to choke on her drink. "What?"

Kilian gave a decided shake of his head. "Absolutely not."

Helena pointed a finger at him. "Listen here, my little reindeer friend."

"I thought we established there is nothing little about me," Kilian said, and drank, holding her dark gaze.

Helena seemed taken aback, impressed with his retort, but then plowed on. "Regardless. My sister has clearly fallen for this prince."

"Crown prince," Lia amended.

"Whatever. You love him. I see it in your face. You're—different. And I'm not going to spend the next hundred years of our lives having you steep with regret."

"Humans don't live that long," Kilian said.

"And you do?" Gracie asked, a little bolder.

He flashed a cocky half smile, his strange green eyes flicking toward her lips. "I'm five hundred and three."

Gracie blinked. Lia couldn't be sure if he was telling the truth, but she was too busy shifting a plan in her mind. She had her sisters, which she'd desperately needed. Never in a million years would she have asked them to go with her. But they'd come with her across the world, and now they would even follow her into another realm. The possibility bloomed in her heart.

"I know. Pros and cons time." Helena clapped her hands. She rounded the kitchen and shortly returned with Lia's stationery. Her notebook and bag of pens.

With her supplies set before her, Lia's fingers twitched. She flipped through the pages. Top ten fantasy romance novels. Top ten Chris Pine movies. Top 100 songs to play at my wedding. Sixteen worst restaurants in the city.

She turned to a clean page, uncapped her pen, and wrote one thing.

Alexander

She didn't need a list. She simply needed a way to get to him.

The three Espinoza sisters turned to the Elfenhörn sitting at their kitchen table. He stopped halfway from his drink and realized what they were getting at.

"Absolutely not. The Nikolas was murdered. His bride usurped the throne. Alexander has returned to face all of it. The Saint only knows if it's safe for three humans to travel there. I won't do it."

The door rang with their pizza. Gracie went off to pay. As Helena leaned forward to stare at Kilian, Lia had a sneaking suspicion that she was going to get her way. Helena always got her way.

"We'll just see about that," she said.

22

ALEXANDER

As they breached the Hallowed Path and entered the expanse of the forest, Alexander trekked in disbelief that he was going to do it. He was returning to the Eternal Winter Forest. For a real, dark moment, he half wanted a shadow sylph to emerge and devour him. Then, and only then, would it be over.

But then he thought of Lia. His sunshine Lia. His darling Lia. His wicked love. He found the strength to walk through the dense, rocky forest, the earth rumbling. It sensed intruders, and they walked faster.

Once they passed the line of trees that marked the forest's end, Alexander inhaled the dry, frigid air. He inhaled so deeply it hurt. He wanted it to hurt. He *deserved* to hurt because he'd left Lia behind. The barest comfort was that he trusted Kilian with his life and knew his friend would reunite her with her sisters.

"Tell me, brother," Hans said, resting a hand on the pommel of his sword. It felt strange to have it at his hip once again. "What was so special about her?"

"You wouldn't understand, as you love no one but yourself."

THE HEART OF WINTER

Hans flashed a cold smile. "Right you are."

Hans's golden steed was hitched to a tree, eating berries from the spindly branches. Its mane was braided with threads of silver. The breed had been Hans's own alchemy, his attempt at creating the fastest horses in the kingdom. This had been the first one to survive to adulthood, and was perhaps the only creature Hans loved.

Alexander mounted the saddle behind his brother. He looked out at the mountain ridge, the winding path with the shimmering palace glinting in the distance. The sun was encroaching toward the horizon.

"We won't make it," Alexander said.

"Ye of little faith, Alexander. I will get you to the seal, and you will claim your birthright, and we will toast at midnight." Hans clicked his tongue, and the horse reared into a gallop, riding so fast Alexander felt the very ground tremble with every pound of the beast's hooves.

They crossed the ice plains and surrounding hills covered in layers of snow. Most of the scenery melted into the speed of the wind. Alexander knew it well. He'd spent years trekking every inch of the kingdom he could, finding a way to connect his heart to the legacy he was supposed to love. One that didn't love him back.

As they entered the city gates, night fell. Alexander noticed the eerie silence first. The streets were still empty. He reminded himself that time had passed for him, like a glamor only he could see. But since then, the people of the kingdom had remained in their homes, hiding from the chaos that had erupted in the palace.

A windowpane slammed shut as they rode past. He saw the head of a woman peek from a tavern then duck back inside. Hooves pounded the cobblestone streets, each clap resonating deep in his bones.

Then they skidded across the frost covering the palace courtyard, and Alexander shouted at his brother to stop.

Bodies, cold and blue, lay with arrows sticking out of their eyes, hearts, legs. A fine layer of frost covered their skin.

Hans reared the horse to a halt. "Celeste has the guard wrapped around her gold-tipped finger. I gave her those golden nails. Now, let's hurry."

"You said she only wanted me." Alexander swung off the steed. He ran and knelt before an all too familiar face.

Elowen.

He'd been in her cabin. He'd drunk her wine and eaten her reserves. He'd fucked Lia in every room. And the whole time, Elowen had been lying there, bleeding. A ragged cry left his body and shook him.

"My prince," Elowen croaked.

"She's alive," Alexander said, putting pressure around the wound in her belly. "Help me."

"We don't have time. We must get to the gardens, to the seal. Alexander!"

Hans grabbed his brother by the collar and yanked at him with a desperation Alexander had never seen from the man. Alexander turned around and swung. Hans's head snapped back, and he fell, landing on a body that was nearly purple with frost.

The sun was about to set. Alexander remembered his own panic at the cabin, and Lia soothing him. They had time. They had time.

Alexander returned to Elowen and carefully assessed the wound.

"Let me," he said, gently removing her palms from her belly. He unbuttoned the embroidered overcoat and pushed up the tunic. Her eyes began to flutter shut.

"I was in your cabin," Alexander confessed. Elowen made a

sound of acknowledgment. That's what Alexander wanted. To keep her awake. To pull her back to the living. "I ate all your beets and cherries. Drank all your whisky. You must stay awake, do you understand? Otherwise, I won't be able to repay you."

Elowen snorted then sobbed through her pain.

Alexander pressed his hand to the gash, likely a sword wound. Her eyes rolled to the back of her head again, lashes fluttering.

"*Forgive* me, Elowen," Alexander begged. He shut his eyes and latched on to the power he'd rejected. The very strength that coursed through his veins. The whispers of a long-gone saint who performed miracles. And yet, it was when he thought of Lia that the power had something to latch on to. Lia who talked so fast and kissed so hard and whimpered so sweetly. Lia who made his magic wild and strange. He harnessed it and felt the gash stitching together like a quilt of sinew and flesh. His palm left a gold print there, and for the stretch of a moment, she was still.

So still, he thought he was too late.

Then Elowen breathed sharply and turned on to her side to cough, her body shivering. "You ate my cherries?"

Alexander pulled her into an embrace, spreading warmth through her body. This time, as the Mark of the Saint burned its way around his clavicle, he didn't mind the sting. "I will make things right, old friend."

"I'll hold you to it." She clapped him on his arm. "Celeste. She's searching for you. She called for your head. Everyone who opposed her—" Her eyes fell to the bodies on the floor.

"Alexander!" Hans shouted. "She's alive, leave her. Let's *go*."

Above, dark clouds amassed over the palace.

"Get to safety," Alexander told Elowen.

Thunder rattled as he pushed to his feet and ran down the

narrow path to the gardens. Lightning crackled and struck the grounds, illuminating the dark.

"We're too late," Hans said, running at Alexander's side.

"Whatever happened to me having little faith?"

Hans grunted. "That was before you had to stop and—"

Hail the size of marbles pelted them. One got Hans on his cheek, drawing blood. Alexander put all his strength into his legs. He slipped on the ice that covered the stone courtyard but kept pushing. Never in any of the records he'd read had there been mention of a hailstorm at the time of the coronation of a Nikolas.

When the maze hedges came into view, Alexander was almost relieved. He'd made it.

He stumbled onto the marble floor, the seal of his ancestor carved in sweeping lines and runes that matched the ink on his body. He peeled off his tunic and sank to his knees. The Mark of the Saint was nearly complete, adorning both his arms. All that was missing was the heart at the center.

And the he said the words his brother didn't get to speak. The words his ancestors had each claimed at the very spot, biding their bodies to the land.

"I am the heart of winter."

He felt magic carve up his skin, but pain slammed into his chest as the Mark stopped. Instead of the warmth he'd become accustomed to, there was resistance, and a hollow cold.

"Hans!" Alexander panted as hail pelted his skin into bruises. He'd never been trained for the moment, not like Will had been. He'd said the right words but it wasn't working. "Why isn't it working? I don't know what to do—"

"Why, you bow, Alexander," a clipped, regal voice said.

Still on his knees, Alexander snapped in her direction. Torches ignited in a row, making shadows dance around Celeste, his brother's murderer. Her gown billowed in the

THE HEART OF WINTER

biting wind, deep ice blue against her snow-white skin. Her eyes were amethyst, unnatural even for the people of the kingdom. There was red in her hair, like she'd wiped her forehead and dragged her husband's blood—or some other poor soul's—across it and forgotten.

Alexander counted half of the king's guard standing at attention behind her, waiting, waiting.

"Why are you doing this?" he asked.

"You'll see. Perhaps you'll even be happy that I have freed you," Celeste said. "I've known you all my life, Alexander. I know how much of a burden this family has been for you."

"All my life?" Alexander scoffed as he stood. "You were my brother's bride for two years. You don't know me at all."

She moved closer. Neither hail nor rain touched her. She smiled the bewitching smile that had mesmerized her brother. "I knew you well enough to find the perfect distraction for you the night of the banquet. I knew that you'd run. But I never expected you to access your power so deeply or even return. I'm curious. Whatever changed your mind?"

"Why don't we talk about this with a nice cup of tea?" Hans offered. He raised a scarred palm at her.

"What will you do, brother," she taunted him. "Turn me to gold?"

Celeste wagged her fingers like she was playing the harp and lightning struck at Hans's feet.

"Aldred," she said.

A guard stepped forward. Alexander knew him. He was one of the Elfenhörn, sworn to the crown, like Kilian had been. He removed his breastplate, his chainmail, his tunic.

"What are you doing?" Alexander drew his sword and took a step forward but the lightning struck him. He felt the current splinter in his veins. There was darkness. His heart stopped. For a moment, there was nothing, and then a rush of cold. He gasped for air, his muscles seizing as he tried to stand.

Aldred shifted into a reindeer with russet fur and antlers etched with runes.

Every muscle in Alexander's body constricted with cramps as he tried to stand. But he couldn't get up. Could barely uncurl his fingers from the trembling fists against his chest.

Celeste withdrew a dagger, crystal and thin, like a long spindle. In a swift thrust, she pierced it through Aldred's throat. Blood flowed from the reindeer and into the grooves of the marble seal.

It was a door.

Cavern, Hans had said.

There was the sound of ancient stone moving, opening up. The hail stopped.

Alexander had left the Eternal Winter Forest to save it from himself, to release it from the line of Nikolas. But he never wanted this. He stared at the parting clouds that opened to show pitch-black sky. There were no stars. Lia had loved stars.

"Rise, Horned King," Celeste whispered.

Feeling returned to him, and he pushed trembling limbs to a stand. Alexander staggered back, searching for his brother, who was slowly retreating to the safety of the hedges. Their dark green leaves never turned during winter.

The earth shook, and even the guard had to catch their balance. Celeste fell to the mouth of the open seal. Her dress pooled like an ocean around her.

From the bowels of the cavern rose a man. Alexander registered the black horns protruding from his temples and sweeping back to sharp points. An unruly black beard. Long raven hair matted with sweat and dirt.

At the center of his chest was the Mark of the Saint, or rather, part of it. The missing part that should have finished at

Alexander's heart. The muscles of the horned man's chest expanded as he leaned his face to the night sky, as if fascinated by it. How long had it been since he'd seen it? How long had he been down there? He took a deep breath, relishing in the open air. His biceps flexed as he extended a hand to help Celeste to her feet. She held out a robe for him, and he stepped into it.

Alexander chanced another step forward. He should run. He should take Hans and go. Find a way to save the people from whatever Celeste had unleashed. But he kept advancing.

"Alexander…" Hans bleated.

The horned man's attention snapped away from the sky. He spoke a single word. "Alex?"

That face. He could have sworn. But no—

The horned man had an aquiline nose, a dusting of freckles that reached even the fringes of his beard. A red eye, like a garnet, and the other nearly black.

"What?" the horned god said, his voice hoarse from disuse. The wrong note on a harp. "Don't you recognize me, cousin?"

"Kit?" Alexander couldn't breathe. Couldn't breathe. He'd dreamed of him every night in the cabin.

Not a dream.

"How?" Alexander seethed, turning to Hans. "Why was he down there?"

"It doesn't matter how," Celeste said.

"Of course it matters!" Alexander shouted. "They told me he was dead."

She offered Kit her spindle dagger. "Kill him."

Kit raised the dagger to his nose. Blood was still dried on it, and he licked it.

Alexander dropped to his knees. Kit had lived. His cousin had lived imprisoned for decades, right beneath his feet. Another sin. Another thing he needed to add to his long list of atonements.

But as he waited for the strike, Kit dropped the blade. The crystal shattered.

"What are you doing?" Celeste grit out. "I killed the king. There are only two left."

Kit raised his fingers slowly. Sharp claws tipped black raked the air. Celeste fell silent. "I was in the caverns for twenty-two years, my dear sister. I have dreamt of the ways I would destroy the kingdom. But I want the heirs of Saint Nikolas to watch."

"Sister?" Hans asked.

Celeste blinked, and her amethyst eyes turned a pale honey, like Alexander's own. Like his mother—and his aunt. The aunt who'd died of heartbreak when Kit had never been found, lost to the forest.

"Seraphina." Alexander spoke the name and watched her wince. "You left."

"I ran," she corrected, her words full of rage. "I saw what they did to my brother. I saw when they brought him back in the dead of night and stuffed him below this seal. My own mother wouldn't believe me. So I ran and vowed to return when I could wield enough power to free Christopher."

"The people you've killed are innocent," Alexander said.

"*I* was innocent." Her eyes were glassy with an anger he knew too well. "Brother, kill him. Or I will."

"Do it, Kit." Alexander straightened on his knees. He tilted his head back for a final strike. It was what he deserved.

"Don't call me that," the horned man said. Beneath the beard and horns, the tail that flicked at the hem of his robe, Alexander wanted to believe that his cousin was still there. "I stopped being a child long ago."

"Christopher," he tried again. "Kill me if you must. But I will not defend myself against your blow. I owe you a life. My life."

Kit—Christopher smiled slowly. "Dramatic as ever, it seems."

"I brought you back to be *king*," Celeste—Seraphina—said. "If you don't kill him, I will. And the other one, too."

Behind them, Hans was hiding in the hedges.

"You heard him. His life is mine." Christopher tilted his face to the rising moon, a veil of red over its usual silver light. "But I will decide the punishment. Come."

"Come where?" Seraphina asked.

"If I am to be king, I want to meet my subjects. The Eternal Winter Forest was founded on the miracles of Saint Nikolas, wasn't it? It is time they knew the true history of this land. Let's start now."

Alexander tracked his cousin's slow movements, like he was used to sitting still for long periods of time. Twenty-two years. He'd been prisoner for twenty-two years. And for what?

"Tell me, Master of Alchemy," Christopher raised his voice to make sure Hans heard him. "Tell us the truth of this kingdom."

"He can't speak the words," Alexander said.

Christopher's red eye pulsed with red light. "Oh, he can. It would hurt him, but you *can* heal him, can't you? Come out, Cousin Hansel!" he growled. "Or I will fetch you. It has been ages since I've run through these gardens."

Hans crept out of the hedges, hatred twisting his mouth. He sidled up behind Alexander.

"Speak."

Hans looked at his brother, his estranged cousins. He didn't seem surprised to see Christopher. Answers swept through Alexander. Because if Hans knew, then so had their brother and their father. They had all known and let Alexander believe that his foolish choices had led to Kit's death.

"S*peak*, brother," Alexander growled.

"When Saint Nikolas was made king by the Elfenhörn, he combined his own power with the land. A land he'd always dreamt of. Full of goodness." Hans stopped, his voice scratching as he coughed. "Virtuous. Devoid of the evil of humanity."

"Do go on," Christopher said, but there was no mirth in his voice. "How did the great *Saint* Nikolas, the Master of Miracles, blessed by God and the heavens, how did he make sure his kingdom remained devoid of evil?"

"He," Hans coughed. "He made an anchor." Hans doubled over, clutching the ground. When he coughed, blood sprayed the snow.

"An anchor for what?" Kit's eyes flamed, his voice taunting as he pounded the ground at Hans's face.

"To harness every impulse, every dark deed and dark heart into a vessel."

By his last word, Hans's voice was a pathetic whisper. Alexander realized that he'd never seen his brother cry before.

Perhaps that was why he got to his knees and healed his brother. This time, he didn't feel the Mark burn. The Mark of the Saint *was* complete. Split between Alexander and Kit.

"Thank you," Hans croaked.

"Don't thank me yet." Alexander's voice was cutting.

"Don't be too cross with him," Kit—Christopher—said. "He's doing what our family has always done."

Seraphina spit at the ground. "Hoard power."

"Please," Alexander begged. "The people are innocent."

"Again with that." Seraphina laughed darkly. "This is the end, Alexander."

"Ki—Christopher," Alexander tried again. "We are not our fathers. We can make it so that what happened to you never happens again. I never wanted this. You more than anyone know that."

Christopher nodded and closed his eyes to the moon again.

Alexander wondered what his cousin felt after so many years underground, feeding on every dark impulse with a magic so deep it utterly transformed him into this.

"I do know," he said softly. "I know that you are a good man. You were always good. You were like my brother. But if you won't help me, then I fear there is only one thing left for me to do."

Christopher was lean but incredibly strong. He grabbed Hans by the throat and threw the Golden Prince into the mouth of the cavern, then turned to Alexander. There was the briefest moment of hesitation before crushing a fist around his cousin's throat.

"I wish it could be another way," said the Horned King. "I really did miss you, brother."

Then he threw Alexander into the deep and shut the way out.

23
LIA

Lia couldn't have known that she followed in the same steps as her beloved, but she already felt closer to him.

Saddled snugly on Kilian's back, the Espinoza sisters made their way through the Hallowed Path and across the forest. The night was dark, and the flashlights they'd brought along barely cut through the pitch-black night.

Kilian's eyes glowed, and Helena made a joke about the reindeer's lack of a red nose. They laughed until there was a hard crunch in the distance. Kilian came to a stop and stomped in a circle, the sisters clinging together, three hearts racing in sync as even Helena remained quiet.

"Something's out there," Gracie said. "I hear singing."

Lia couldn't hear anything but the beat of her fear and Kilian's hooves as he resumed cutting through the dark wood. Goosebumps puckered across her body despite the insulated warmth of her coat and the wool hat that covered her ears.

As they reached the end of the forest, they stopped for a rest. The moon shone down on a wide plain of snow, casting a ruby glow on the sprawling alien landscape. Undulating hills split by a long road, and there—in the horizon—was the palace, glinting like a jewel.

"A red moon," Gracie whispered, holding tightly to Lia's waist. "That's never good, is it?"

Kilian shook his snout, panting hard. He must have been so tired, carrying the three of them. Lia was grateful for him and would have to find a way to thank him for letting them bully him into taking them to find Alexander.

"Are you sure you can't hear that?" Gracie asked.

"Maybe we should go," Helena said.

Kilian's head snapped back toward the forest. The reins tugged out of Lia's hands. She knew something was wrong, felt the ripple of the night, followed by Gracie's scream. The reindeer bucked violently as the very ground undulated, and they were thrown off the saddle.

Lia fell hard and heard something break. Her flashlight landed in the distance, and she tried to crawl to it. Vertigo overpowered her senses as the earth trembled.

When her hand closed on the flashlight, she aimed it at the forest. The moss underbelly beneath the trees had opened, roots dangling like severed tendons. Deep within, incandescent blue and green flames danced. The stench of sulfur and rot hit Lia's nose. Music, haunting and slow, filtered out.

And then, it was gone.

The trees were silent, leaves rustling to the ground.

Lia shone her flashlight in a circle. "Helena! Gracie?"

"Here," Helena groaned. She was several feet away, cradling her arm. Lia went to her, but her eldest sister only shook her off. "I'm fine. It's just a little a sprain."

Kilian had transformed back into his human form, his naked skin red under the strange moonlight, and his eyes still retained the reindeer glow.

"Gracie?" Helena's voice warbled.

There was the scuff of boots on the ground, the howl of some unseen creature in the dark. Lia heard her own panting, the scream in her blood as she spun and spun but didn't see her sister.

"Gracie!" she shouted.

"Graciela!"

"They took her," Kilian said. "Under the hill. The forest is awake."

"What the *fuck* does that mean?" Helena shouted.

Kilian picked up his satchel and yanked on his clothes. "It means whatever happened to Alexander is worse than I imagined."

"*Where* is Gracie?" Lia said. This couldn't be happening. What had she expected? Fairy tales, the old ones, never ended happily. Fuck Disney for twisting her perception of happy endings. "Who took her?"

"The Elfenhörn," Kilian explained. "The ones who still live under the hill. The ones who did not bend to the Saint. If they're awake, that means something has happened to Alexander."

A pressure built in Lia's belly. Alexander had to be all right. He had to be. But Gracie— "Aren't they your people? We can just explain what's happening and ask them to give her back."

As her eyes acclimated to the strange red glow from the moon, she saw Kilian retrieving a small dagger and tucking it in his belt. "You have to keep going. Alexander needs you, perhaps now more than ever. I will get your sister back."

"No," Lia cried. How could she choose between Alexander and her sister? Two pieces that made up her entire heart. "Helena, go with him."

"And leave you alone?" Helena had her arms wrapped around herself. Her teeth chattered in the icy wind. "Fuck. Fuck this."

"I will bring Graciela back to you," Kilian said. His eyes relaxed into their pale green irises. "I swear it on my life. The heart of the forest does not like strangers. It will be better for her if I go alone."

Behind her, Helena screamed into the night. Lia faced the dark forest. On the outside of it, the wall of impenetrable ancient trees made her shudder. If she went to Alexander, perhaps he could get Gracie back. The ferocity in Kilian's gaze convinced her that his vow was true. It was the only reason she relented.

"Bring her back," Lia whispered. "Please."

"My word is my bond." He took Lia's palm and brought it to his forehead. There, the outline of a leaf etched itself in gold, then sank into his skin. A magical vow.

She didn't want to ask what would happen to him, if he failed.

With Kilian's instructions, Lia and Helena began their trek to the palace. It was simple. There was one long road. They glanced back to watch Kilian disappear into the trees and forged ahead, stopping only twice to rest their feet and warm their bodies with the flask of whisky in Helena's jacket. They didn't speak of Gracie, but Helena, who never cried, wept in defiant silence all the way. Lia was in too much shock and forced herself to keep it together. For Helena. For Gracie. For Alexander. The wind felt like fists punching against their chests. But step by step, blister by blister, and every shed tear, the two Espinoza sisters reached the empty village.

Every window was shuttered. Not a single soul attempted to peek at the strangers heading to the palace.

When they reached the gates, Lia thought it was the most

beautiful structure she'd ever seen. Twisting spires and arched windows with colored glass. Columns that reminded her of the Greek wing of the Metropolitan Museum of Art, and touches of old cathedrals, somehow melded into one.

As the sun rose high beyond the clouds and surrounding mountains, Lia squinted against the light. A sound broached the eerie silence. The solemn notes of a cello along with a voice that made Lia think of funerals.

Lia noticed scarlet patches on the ground, and if she relaxed her eyes, she thought she could see the outlines of bodies in the snow, like dead angels. Fear tightened in her gut. Alexander. Where was Alexander?

"Let's see what all the noise is about." Helena forged on like she was the queen of the palace.

Inside, the halls were richly trimmed in gold. She saw Hans's touch in the gaudy ceilings, which reminded her of the summer she'd visited the Vatican for a college art class. There were portraits of the old kings, queens, and other royals. They followed the undulating warble of a soprano into an empty ballroom.

Their boots echoed sharply. Helena yanked off her hat, shook the frost from her coat, and spun with her eyes trained on the painted ceiling. The art depicted a severe man who must have been the first Saint Nikolas shining a beam of light over a thousand reindeer, hawks, and all sorts of creatures.

"Good thing we're here. Your kingly boyfriend does *not* know how to throw a party. This place is dead."

Before Lia could chide her for using humor to deflect, a low, rumbling laughter echoed behind them.

"How very right you are," the deep voice said.

The Espinoza sisters turned to find a man upon a golden throne. He wore a silk robe the color of the night sky, dotted with constellations of gold thread. It was open to reveal lean muscles and a tuft of dark hair curling over his pectorals and leading to a single trail that vanished into low-slung leather pants. His horns gleamed like polished tourmaline, and he leaned like he was bored, a long black claw clenched his teeth as he assessed them.

At his side was a startlingly beautiful young woman with the same honey-colored eyes as Alexander. Her light brown hair tumbled in ringlets, and a crown of gold branches adorned her head. She did not sit, and Lia thought she had the air of a woman who was not to be fucked with.

"Is this—?" Helena began to ask, still walking toward the throne like she was magnetized.

Lia grabbed her sister by the arm and yanked her back. "He's not Alexander."

"I know you," the horned man said, sitting forward with deep interest. "I've seen you in Alexander's dreams."

"Dreams?" the beautiful woman and Lia said at the same time.

"You never said anything about dreams," the woman pressed.

"You didn't ask," the horned man said, a tinge of annoyance in his clipped words. "Do behave, Seraphina. We have guests."

"Where is Alexander?" Lia demanded.

The singer in the corner cracked on a note, like he was scared for her.

"Would you like to join him?" the horned man asked, taunting her. His single red iris flashed like the core of a ruby.

"What did you do to him?" Lia balled her hands into fists, useless against horns and claws, but her anger didn't let her think.

"Not enough," Seraphina muttered.

Helena stepped in front of Lia and stomped to the dais,

only stopping when she was mere feet from him. "Listen, your horny majesty—"

He let loose a low growl.

"I've had two sisters kidnapped in the span of forty-eight hours. We got attacked by a tree. My feet hurt after walking more miles than I have in my entire life, and I'm pretty sure I lost a toe to frostbite. I was expecting a fucking medieval castle with a giant feast, but your party is so dead, I'm about to write you a eulogy. So if you'd be so kind as to tell my sister where her boyfriend is, I would really appreciate it."

The music scratched to a stop. Seraphina was practically frothing at the mouth.

The horned man's red iris flared. He radiated power. The Mark, so much like the tattoo on Alexander, was etched in inky tendrils over his heart. Lia held her breath for the claws to strike.

Instead, he prowled off his throne and towered over Helena. He walked with his hands at his back, taking his sweet time. The tie around his robe came undone and the garment slipped haphazardly off one shoulder, exposing the deep cuts of his shoulders and the grooves of his Adonis muscles.

Lia noticed Helena's poker face break ever so slightly. Her sister blinked and her nostrils flared. Signs that only Lia would notice.

Slowly, he raised a long nail to a damp curl resting over Helena's cheekbone. He entwined it around the black tip and carefully moved it to the side.

"And what will you give me for reuniting your sister with her true heart?" The words were rough and low. Lia felt them in her belly.

"Depends." Helena blinked again but squared her shoulders. "What do you want?"

The horned man grinned, and even Lia had to admit how

intoxicating he was. Too-sharp canines and a full mouth beneath that trim black beard. He leaned into Helena's ear, pitching his voice low enough that all Lia could hear was susurration.

Helena didn't betray any emotion. She'd regained hold of her steel. It worried Lia. What had he asked of her?

"Deal." She spat on her palm and extended it to the horned man.

He took her hand, but instead of shaking it, he kissed here right there at the center, his tongue following in one long stroke. Then he turned his multicolored eyes to Seraphina and said, "Open the seal. I must retrieve Alexander."

Lia's heart swelled with emotion and relief. Alexander. She was going to see her Alexander. All she needed was Gracie's safe return, and everything would be all right. But one look at Seraphina, and Lia's hope was tempered.

"I brought you back to destroy him, not reunite him with his little pet."

Helena whirled on the beautiful woman.

Lia held her back. "Enough."

"Seraphina," the horned man warned. "Helena here is going to be my Master of Revels. I cannot corrupt the Eternal Winter Forest if they're too afraid to leave their houses, can I?"

Seraphina only narrowed her gaze at her brother, but she didn't correct him. "As you wish, *Your Majesty*."

24
ALEXANDER

Alexander did not pace. Did not scream. Did not beat his brother to a bloody pulp. Did not even try to break his way out of their prison.

Instead, in the dark of the cavern beneath the palace, Alexander, heir of the Nikolas, deposed king of the Eternal Winter Forest, remembered. He remembered his last day with Kit. Christopher.

They'd gone so deep into the Elfenhörn Forest, in the parts forbidden to all. Then they'd fallen through a hole in the ground. When Alexander got free, scrambling out of the pit, he couldn't reach his cousin's hand. Instead, he tried branches, vines. Everything snapped and broke.

"Go," Kit had said. "Get help and come back. Please."

By the time Alexander had reached the palace and told every adult he could, he was exhausted. His uncle, the Master of Alchemy then, closed himself in counsel with the king. And when Alexander woke up, the kingdom was in mourning.

Now, in the underground caverns, Alexander dug into his pocket and withdrew a tiny ornament, cradling the Santa Claus in his palm. He'd taken it before he left Lia behind. Lia. His

THE HEART OF WINTER

Lia. What a fool he'd been. All he had left of her was a wooden toy.

If he couldn't have her and the brief life he'd dreamt with her, then at the very least, he could finally get answers from his brother.

"You let me believe Kit was dead," Alexander said.

Hans, who was at the top of the spiral steps, used his power to turn the stone to gold.

"Are you *decorating* the lock?"

"I'm trying to change its composition so it becomes easier to lift."

"Don't we need a sacrifice?" Alexander shut his eyes against the memory of the Elfenhörn bleeding out. He couldn't stop it. He'd never been witness to so much bloodshed before. But he also couldn't deny he was glad his cousin was free.

"We are not the anchor to the kingdom's sins," Hans ran agitated fingers through his hair. His voice had taken on a scratchy tone, like he had smoked havengrass since birth. "But it can't be opened from down here. Curse the Saint, this place smells."

"It's almost like a boy has lived here since he was thirteen," Alexander offered darkly.

"He was fed and clothed, though he doesn't seem to like wearing them. I don't know why you're the one who's cross. I should be angry with you. You left your pretty little human to do one thing and, in the end, you were a coward. You failed."

"Come down here and say those things to my face."

Hans snarled in his brother's direction. "And you wonder why Father had no patience for you. Your answer to everything was brute strength. Anger. Lashing out. You never even tried to—"

"Be good?"

"To fit, Alexander. You never tried to fit in this family. And now, the kingdom is in ruins. Don't forget, *I* didn't create this."

Alexander wanted to laugh. His entire family had conspired to take away devious impulses from every living person, and damned who knew how many souls to a fate worse than death. They were to blame. They were the rotten thing in the realm.

"It should have been you," Alexander snarled.

"Actually, it was supposed to be you." Hans spoke the words with a terrible cough at the end. He spit a wad of dark blood.

Alexander ascended the steps one by one, until his hair grazed the top of the seal, and he grabbed his brother by his collar. He squeezed his throat. "*What* did you say?"

"I didn't mean it."

Alexander had the urge to shake his brother, crush his face until he stopped being so perfect. He wasn't used to such a violent impulse, even when his brothers had been the utmost cruel. It startled him into letting Hans go.

In that moment, the seal opened. Kit crouched above them. His dual-colored eyes were surprised to find the brothers at the top of the steps.

"Your presence is requested," he said to Alexander.

"By whom?" he asked.

Kit gave no indication of answering, only stood, his robe ties fluttering in Alex's face. "If you want to stay here…"

Alex scrambled and climbed out. Hans tried to follow, but Christopher gave him a shove. "Not you."

The seal shut, and Hans's screams trailed them until they were back inside.

The palace was eerily quiet. Alexander couldn't remember the last time he'd seen an empty palace. No courtiers. No villagers walking the gardens. No Will stalking the corridors with his princess at his side. A princess who had turned out to be their cousin—Seraphina. Alexander's mind spun.

At the very least, he was free. Perhaps he could convince Kit to put a stop to his sister's machinations.

"Where are you taking me?"

The Horned King said nothing, but Alexander still followed down the twisting corridors he knew all too well. They came to a stop at his own chambers.

"I expect you at the banquet tonight." His cousin watched him with a mischievous grin. What was he playing at?

"Kit—"

"Don't," he said, snarling to reveal a canine so sharp, Alexander wondered how it didn't shred the inside of his lip. "I stopped being Kit in that cavern. Now. A guard will fetch you tonight."

Without another answer, the Horned King was gone.

Alexander opened the door and stepped into his chambers. The living space was the same as always, brown leather and dark wood. He had never let Hans turn his bedroom into a hideous gold-trimmed nightmare.

He went directly to the bar, and grabbed the first bottle without thinking. As he poured himself a glass, Alexander felt something in the room with him. Someone. Had Christopher led him to his own death? Seraphina? God, she'd been their *cousin*. Whatever was waiting for him, it was what he deserved.

He turned to meet his fate, and when he did, he dropped his glass. Whisky spilled on his bare feet. Glass nicked at his skin.

"Lia?" He stepped back. "It's a trick. It's Seraphina's sorcery."

Her hair fell in windswept tangles. Her cheeks were still pink from the cold. Had she traveled all the way here? *How* had she done it?

"It's me." So soft he couldn't be sure if he'd imagined it.

Alexander advanced slowly, the hateful wretched thing in his heart twisting because he did not deserve her. He did not deserve to feel this happy when his kingdom was broken and his cousin, the only person he'd truly considered a brother, had been utterly changed.

He fell at her feet, elated that he wasn't imagining things. That she was there with him. He kissed her stomach. He kissed her heart. He kissed her breasts and the bare tender spot of her neck until he reached her lips. He was so hard from touching her, smelling the flower oils and salt on her skin.

"What happened to you?" she asked, taking his face in her soft palms.

He shook his head. He couldn't speak about it yet.

"Later." She soothed him with a kiss.

"How did you get here?" he asked.

She pressed a finger to his lips then shed her coat. Undid his trousers, running a hard palm over his erection. "Later."

"Fuck, Lia. I am so sorry. I am so sorry."

She rucked his trousers down his hips. "You left me."

"I thought I was doing the right thing." The last thing he wanted to give her was excuses. Not when he ached for her. "Forgive me."

She seized his cock with her fists and teased the head with her thumb. She was going to torture him as punishment. He gave a thrust of his hips and nearly came right then and there.

"You left me, and I thought I'd never see you again. Never get to tell you that I love you."

He grabbed her by her shoulders and gathered her into his arms. He picked her up and sat her on the long wooden table strewn with fountain pens, a vase of dead flowers, books he'd left half open, unfinished like their love.

But he wasn't going to run away from her, not ever again.

She raised her hands, and he undressed her, freeing her of her strange tunic and divesting her of her black leggings. Her underthings had tiny boughs of holly and candy canes printed on them.

The sight of them, of the triangle of her pussy outlined by the flimsy fabric, made him wild. He barely had them off her legs before he was parting her with his tongue. The sweet, wet taste of her made him harder than ever.

"Please," she moaned.

He stroked the most vulnerable part of her, and he had the notion that he could die right then and there with his mouth between her thighs.

"Alexander, I need you inside of me." She trailed her hands across his shoulders, guiding him back up.

She parted her legs, so exposed. So trusting. She didn't know what he'd done. She didn't know what he was responsible for. But he couldn't deny her, and he was a wretched beast of a man because he wanted her more than anything.

With her still sitting on the table, they kissed, fast and desperate. Both of them scared that they'd be torn apart any minute. She seized his shaft, and nocked his aching cock like an arrow at her entrance.

He stretched her open in a brutal thrust. She tugged him closer, raking her nails down his back. It was so good. Being inside Lia was so unbelievably good. He had to feel the sensation of entering her again, so he pulled out.

She whimpered and scooted forward on the table, clinging to his shoulders for support. Together, they watched him enter her again and again. Every time he slid in a little deeper, rutted a little harder.

He felt the pressure in his lower belly gather and draw down. He crawled on top of her, fucking her to the hilt. Fucking her until he saw the spark of pleasure in her eyes. Recognized the way she bit her bottom lip and searched for his friction. Her legs wrapped around his waist and pinned him impossibly tight.

"Don't leave me again," she told him.

He rested his hand on her chest, putting pressure on her throat as she ground her heels into his ass. They were as close as two people could be, and it wasn't enough. It would never be enough because he loved her more than his kingdom, more than his own worthless life.

"Never again. You're mine, Lia," he growled as her walls tightened around him. "Marry me, my darling. Be mine forever."

She gasped, her eyes flaring wide as she came wet and whimpering. "Yes! Yes. Of course I'll marry you."

"Fuck," he cursed, her very words tearing the seed from his cock as he pulsed inside her. His Lia. His future bride. "I love you. You are my whole bloody heart."

Together they watched as a thin gold line etched itself around their ring fingers. Engagement vows, like his parents once had. Lia gasped and crushed her lips to his with a kiss.

"I love you, too." Lia smiled, and then her exhaustion overpowered her. How long had it been since she'd slept? She clung to his neck, and he carried her to his bed. The sight of her quickly trailing off into an orgasm-induced sleep filled his heart in a way that ached. He wondered if it would ever stop hurting to want her so much.

As he tucked her under the satin covers, Alexander worried that Christopher had *allowed* her there, in his room. He couldn't be certain what his cousin was planning, but Alexander had to be careful. He thumbed the new mark on his skin, one he relished in bearing. Lia was to be his bride, after all. He'd do anything for her, anything to keep her safe.

Even if it meant standing beside the Horned God and watching the Eternal Winter Forest burn.

EPILOGUE

Helena Espinoza had faced down corrupt landlords trying to make money off disenfranchised tenants. She'd had an angry husband slash her tires and follow her home after she represented the wife suing him for custody of their children. She'd endured learning how to make pork hallacas from her grandmother without complaining that the hot corn meal burned her hands.

Helena had a poker face, not because she liked to gamble, and not because she liked being called cold, hard, *ice princess*. She kept her emotions in check because the world didn't want emotional women. They didn't want women who wept at heartbreak or felt too much in public or in the courtroom. And so she did her best to be made of steel and stone. The only things that could soften her were her sisters.

Gracie was gone—taken. And it was all her fault. She knew Lia would blame herself, but it had been Helena who had convinced them they should take the leap. They were in the kingdom of terrible parties for Alexander, but Helena had wanted to see magic for herself. Lia was too good, too selfless to put anyone ahead of her own wants and needs. That's why Helena had to step in.

And Gracie had paid the price.

Deep in her heart, she knew her sister was alive. Gracie had to be, because Helena didn't know what she would do if something happened to her. All they could do for the moment was trust Kilian. She hoped the reindeer man would keep his word.

Now, she only had to keep hers.

There was a knock at her door, and she answered it. She'd bathed and had accepted the healing balm to mend her wrist sprain but had refused the help of the elvish-looking servant girls. She was a fucking adult and could get dressed on her own. The only problem was she didn't like any of the dresses in the armoire. They just weren't her. She had been so used to power suits and athleisure wear that she never gave a thought to what magical palace banquet attire might look like. Pro-bono work didn't exactly get her invited to galas of the rich and corrupt.

She pulled on a golden number that hugged her long body in all the right curves and made her light brown skin shine. Her hair fell in black waves, and she'd found pots of powders and touched the shimmer to the corners of her eyelids.

"Come in," she said.

Helena expected the servant girls again, or another palace guard. They were more serious than the nutcracker-looking guys at Buckingham Palace from her summer abroad during law school. But when the door opened, it was him.

The Horned King.

He was dressed for dinner, and when he leaned at the threshold to her room, her stomach gave a tiny squeeze. It had been the same feeling as when he'd brushed her cheek with his claw and then whispered their bargain in her ear.

She licked her lips and pulled on her mask of disinterest. "I didn't know kings made house calls."

THE HEART OF WINTER

"I am not a king," he said with an edge to his voice.

"Your girlfriend thinks differently." Her lip curled into a devilish smile despite herself. Fine. She wanted to know what was between him and the bitchy brunette. She did not need a jealous lover putting a hex on her, or whatever they did in this place.

"My sister." His thick black brows knit together. He tugged on his beard but reached lower than where it stopped at his chin, like he was used to it being longer. Somehow, that small movement piqued her interest.

"I hate kings," he said. "I am the un-king."

She fluffed her hair in the tall mirror, watching *him* watching her. "You're anarchy."

"If you're lucky." His eyes swept over her breasts, lingering at the swell of her hips.

"I was born lucky."

"I came to escort you to dinner," he said abruptly. If she didn't know any better, she would have thought he was nervous. How could she, a mere mortal, make a man with horns nervous? "My court manners are rusty, but I know that much."

"You're not wearing your silk robe." She hated that she let her disappointment into her voice.

"Would you like me to slip into it?" His eyes were so unnerving. One sharp like a ruby, and one black like hematite. She wasn't sure if they scared her or thrilled her.

"No, I like this." And she did. His waistcoat was embroidered with black-on-black silk fabric. There was a red ascot at his throat, and his fitted pants hugged his thighs. His tail was the only sign that he wasn't in control. The black tuft twitched as she sauntered across the room.

He offered his hand like a gentleman out of a story book, and Helena smiled at the fact that her nails were just as sharp as his, even if she'd bought hers at the salon before they left for Germany.

"Are you afraid?" he asked as she hesitated to take his hand. The tail swished once. Twice.

"I'm not afraid of anything, *Unking*," she answered honestly. "You're the one who's nervous."

He let a growl escape his throat. "I am simply impatient to start my reign as unking."

"And that's why I'm here," she said, resting her hand on his palm. Slowly, he closed his clawed fingers around hers. The nails were black, bleeding past the nail bed to the soft skin of his digits. Something inside of her tightened with anticipation. What would it feel like to have that hand around her throat? Would he hurt her?

Her pulse fluttered at her clavicle, and lower, as his tail brushed her ankle once. He took a step back, like he hadn't meant to, then squared his shoulders and led her out the door. The corridor was dimly lit with hazy sconces. Gilded-framed paintings of serious faces scowled at them as they made their way to the banquet.

"You're here as agreed upon by our deal," he said. "I know what it's like to be a prisoner, and I have no intention of doing that to you."

"But I am a prisoner," she said. "I can't go home."

"You're my guest. You have the run of the place. No one will harm you or your sisters. I even freed my cousin so he could be reunited with his love."

They turned into another long hall. She was definitely going to need breadcrumbs or some sort of string to get around the labyrinth of the palace.

"For one hundred and one days I am your, uh, what did you call it?"

"Master of Revels," he said and cast a single glance her way.

THE HEART OF WINTER

She did not miss the way he lingered at her the dip of her breasts.

"And that's *all* you expect from me?" she asked, her words heavy with meaning.

"That is all I expect from you," he said softly. "I know I look like a monster, but I would never hurt you."

His words were so full of anguish, cast in a low whisper, that they skated across her skin.

"Well then, I have a lot of work to do for a hundred and one days." She could plan parties and live her best palace life. After that, she and her sisters were free to go, and Alexander and Lia could be together. Besides, she needed as much time as possible to find Gracie. A hundred and one days with the Horned King was worth it just to have her sisters happy, to have her sisters back.

As they stepped into the banquet hall, they were greeted by Seraphina, Lia, and a delicious brooding man dressed in red she could only assume was Alexander.

The Horned King dropped her hand and plopped down at the head of the table, running a clawed hand over his horns.

For a moment, Helena itched to touch them.

"Sit," he commanded.

A slender young man with slightly pointed ears appeared with a bottle of wine, and Helena snatched it from him. When she winked at him, his ruddy cheeks turned scarlet. "Oh, we're going to need many more. And bubbly if you have it."

Helena emptied the wine into their goblets. The Horned God raised his high, eyes trained on her and only her, and said, "Let the debauchery begin."

FIND OUT WHAT HAPPENS TO THE ESPINOZA SISTERS IN...

THE HEART OF SHADOWS

Coming Fall 2022

ABOUT THE AUTHOR

Rizzo Rose has been dreaming up broody heroes as long as she can remember. She loves spiked hot chocolate, fairytales, and thick romance novels. When she's not waiting for her HEA, she's busy writing them for others.

Sign up for her newsletter to be notified of releases, sales, bonus content, and other news!

www.rizzorose.com

Made in the USA
Middletown, DE
15 June 2023